Nicholas
and the
Spirit of Bliss

Nicholas
and the
Spirit of Bliss

Linda Eschler

iUniverse, Inc.
New York Bloomington

Nicholas and the Spirit of Bliss

Copyright © 2009 by Linda Eschler

iUniverse books may be ordered through booksellers or by contacting:
iUniverse
1663 Liberty Drive
Bloomington, IN 47403
www.iuniverse.com
1-800-Authors (1-800-288-4677)

Because of the dynamic nature of the Internet, any Web addresses or links contained in this book may have changed since publication and may no longer be valid. This is a work of fiction. All of the characters, names, incidents, organizations, and dialogue in this novel are either the products of the author's imagination or are used fictitiously.

ISBN: 978-1-4401-9852-6 (pbk)
ISBN: 978-1-4401-9853-3 (ebk)

Printed in the United States of America
iUniverse rev. date: 12/02/09

Introduction

We last saw Nicholas on the Island of Bliss. He, Claire, Geoffrey and Heather had just discovered that they would play a major role in repopulation, after the end of the world, as we know it.

The four of them would take many of the people they had rescued to other places in the world. These people would become the first generation in the new world; a World of Knowing. There would be no doubt, no hate, no jealously. There would be only love.

Now, before they could take others out into the new world, there was a lot they needed to learn. Leo would be their mentor, once again.

You were told in, "Awakening Nicholas," that there would be a time when people did not die. Everyone would be able to project themselves any place they wanted to be. Death would just simply not be necessary in order to be with your loved ones that had crossed over.

But, let's not jump ahead of ourselves. Nicholas and Geoffrey have a much more urgent mission ahead of them.

Chapter One

"I am still reeling from all of this," said Claire. *"First, I find out my parents are not my* parents, but my aunt and uncle, then, I find out that my real parents are some kind of supernatural people. Next, I find out that the man I love is over two hundred years old, and that he is a super hero for eight months of the year, and Santa Claus the other four months."

"Don't forget the rest of the story," said Heather. "These wonderful little children that we have loved for so long, and wanted to protect, could probably take care of us."

Nicholas and Geoffrey began to laugh.

"None of this really makes sense," said Nicholas. "But the fact that every thing is done for love, makes it all right."

"And don't you ladies forget that either," said Geoffrey.

'Is that kind of like Ditto Geoffrey?"

"That is exactly like Ditto, my friend. "Now, if ya

don't mind, Nicholas, I think we need to be heading back to the Main House. Why I can swear I smell Molly's pork chops."

"Let's get together after dinner; we need to discuss how we are going to handle getting ready for Christmas, not to mention our weddings."

"I agree Claire" said Heather. "My parents will be here in a couple of weeks, and the children's parents will be here also. This seems so overwhelming."

"Don't worry, my love," said Geoffrey, "t will all work out."

"Geoffrey is right," said Claire. "Just think, the people that I believed were my parents will be here, and though I love them as if they were my real parents, I also remember Leo and Ciara (French for Claire), as my real parents. I know all of this happened for a reason, so I choose to feel that everything will fall into place."

"You're right, sweetie," said Heather. "The most important thing, to remember, is that we are marrying the most wonderful men in the entire Universe, we live on the most beautiful island in the world, and we get to bake cookies for the elves."

"Look, it's starting to snow again," said Claire. "Can you think of anything more wondrous, than snow for Christmas, on a tropical island?"

"So if we create our own reality," said Nicholas "then we all must have wished for snow at the same time."

"That is too deep for me on an empty stomach," said Geoffrey. "We can resume this conversation after dinner."

Chapter Two

The next morning, Leo asked Nicholas to meet him in the rose garden, after breakfast. "Nicholas, my son," said Leo, "you and Geoffrey are going on a mission but it will be a very short one.

Nicholas knew, for a fact, that Leo must have read his mind, because he never mentioned anything about a mission to Leo. Not that it really mattered, Nicholas knew that Leo was a very big part of the new beginning for the earth, and he considered it a privilege to know Leo, much less be considered a son to him.

"You know whatever plans you have for us, sir, will be carried out without question.

"I know this, Nicholas, and that is what makes this so very hard for me. You and Geoffrey are going back to rescue Geoffrey's mother. This will be a year after Geoffrey's father has crossed over. Geoffrey will be very emotional, so I am depending on you to take care of him this time. I know that you care for Geoffrey as a brother, so I'm sure you have no problem with this, but I have also come to care for Geoffrey as a son."

"Leo, if you don't mind my asking, what is the reason for bringing Geoffrey's mother here?

"Because she is a big part of why Geoffrey is such a beautiful soul, Nicholas; besides, she is grieving herself to death. She had no closure with Geoffrey because he just disappeared from her life, then she lost her husband. I owe this to Geoffrey."

"I understand, Sir."

"Good, now let's find Geoffrey and give him the good news?"

Claire and Heather were in the solarium discussing how they were going to tell the children that they were not orphans after all.

"How in the world can we explain this to them?" asked, Claire. "We can't just walk up to them and say hey kids, guess what? You all have parents, but they have been hiding out on another planet until it was safe to reclaim you. Oh yes, and by the way, all of you are aliens, and have super powers."

Heather began to laugh. "I'm sorry, Claire, it just sounded so much like a …"

"I know, I know," said Claire, as she began to laugh.

"It does sound like some bad sci-fi story but we still have to tell the children the truth and I believe I know just how to do it."

"Remember when I told the children the story about

the little girl on the island, and afterwards told them it was a true story about me.?"

"That is genius, Claire; let's go let them know that there will be a special story time tonight after dinner."

By this time, Leo and Nicholas had found Geoffrey down by the beach with the children. He said they were making the world's first snowman made of sand and snow.

Claire and Heather arrived shortly after.

"Hey guys," said Heather, "do you mind if we help finish the snowman, or sandman, or *whatever* he is?"

"Perfect timing," said Leo. "I have some things to discuss with Nicholas and Geoffrey anyway. Let's go get a cup of Molly's famous hot chocolate, shall we?"

Chapter Three

Everyone gathered at the main house for dinner that evening, and Leo announced that somewhere on the island, there was one particularly large Christmas tree that would be brought to the main house. He said there would be a tree trimming party, and everyone would be expected to attend. He also said that he would like the children to each make an ornament for the tree, and that each year they would place this ornament on the tree.

"This will be the beginning of a tradition for our family, here on the island,"

"Father," said Claire, "that sounds wonderful, and so familiar to me."

"Indeed, my sweetheart," he said. "I still have the ornament you made when you were very young."

"I remember it now mother helped me make it. It was a paper Mache ball, and we hung three little hearts on it. You said that no matter where we were, our hearts would always be close together. In fact, I remember my parents that raised me giving it to me every year to hang on our tree, and telling me that I was the heart in the middle, and someday I would meet the other two hearts. I remember asking questions every year until I guess I figured it was just a childhood fairy tale that I out grew.

I still have the ornament Father; in fact I brought it with me because I knew I would be spending Christmas here on Paradise Island.

The children said that since Claire had made the very first ornament on the island, she should be the first to hang hers on the tree.

"I would be honored children; especially since this would be the first Christmas that the three hearts would be together again."

After dinner, Leo, Nicholas and Geoffrey went into the solarium, so that Claire and Heather could tell the children the real story of their lives.

As Leo poured the three of them a Brandy, he asked Geoffrey why he didn't react when he and Nicholas told him about his father's death, and about the mission to rescue his mother.

"Sir, my parents died long ago. I was very young, but I remember the day that the men came and told me that my parents had been in an accident, and were not coming back. They took me away to live in the castle and trained me to be a knight. I did not want to insult you sir, and that is why I thanked you and excused myself."

"My God, Geoffrey," said Nicholas, "you have not seen your parents since you were a young boy?"

"My parents are dead, Nicholas."

"Geoffrey," said Leo, "you know that I would never lie to you, don't you?"

"Of course, Sir."

"Then I must tell you that your mother is very much alive. Your father passed away about a year ago."

"After you were taken away, your mother was informed of all that was happening in your life, then suddenly a messenger came and said that you were dead and the news broke her heart. Your mother is a wonderful person, Geoffrey, and because of what she taught you in your younger years, you grew into the man that I am proud to call my friend. Your father was a good man as well; however; he was very ill, had been for years and when he finally crossed over, your mother felt as if she was completely alone. This, my friend, is why I chose to bring your mother to the Island of Bliss. You both deserve to be together, and everyone on this island could benefit from knowing your mother."

"But why would they take me away from my parents, it's not as if we were royalty." "But you are indeed royalty," said Leo. "Your mother was Lady Margaret. She lived in the castle, but she fell in love with a commoner. Your mother kept you pretty hidden, but when the prince, to whom your mother was betrothed, found out that she had born a son, he was determined to punish your mother, by taking her only child that he felt should be his. He told King Arthur that Lady Margaret agreed to have her son raised in the castle, so that he could have all that she was unable to offer."

"I do remember a prince that was very kind to me, Prince Andrew. He took me under his wing, and he would tell me that I should think of him as my father.

I cannot believe this, my mother is alive and we will be together again. This is wonderful news, Leo."

"Indeed, my boy, it is wonderful news."

Chapter Four

The next morning, the island was no longer covered in snow. Nicholas and Geoffrey were preparing for their mission, and Claire and Heather were waiting for their parents to arrive.

The story telling had gone very well the night before. By the time Claire and Heather finished the story, the children had figured out that they were the children in the story.

Nicholas and Geoffrey told Claire and Heather about their mission, and Heather was extremely happy that Geoffrey would be reunited with his mother, although she knew that this had been quite a shock for him.

Claire couldn't help but think about Nicholas, and how all of them had their parents, *except* Nicholas. Somehow, it didn't seem quite fair. *She made a mental note to ask Leo why Nicholas had no family.*

As Leo was prepping Nicholas and Geoffrey for the mission, he noticed that the skies were beginning to darken a little more than normal. In fact, this did not look like a storm at all. It looked more like an invasion from the sky.

"Are you two ready for departure?" asked Leo "Ready," said Nicholas. "I think more than ready," said Geoffrey.

As the two men disappeared from Leo's sight, he was still staring at the dark skies, and he knew that this was not only the beginning of the end, but also the beginning of a *new world*.

"Leo," asked Dr. Holiday, as he approached Leo on the front porch, "what is going on tonight in our skies?" "I'm not quite sure, my friend, but it does have me a little troubled."

"You don't think that it could be ..." But before Doc Holiday could finish, Leo said that he didn't see how that was possible, because all of their enemies had destroyed each other out of greed.

"I fear that this is the beginning of the end of the world, as we know it."

"But what about the plans to take some of the island families to other locations; so they will be able to help other families adapt to living on earth, in a *new world*?"

"I don't feel things will move that fast. There will be storms, and fires, and volcanoes, before the end, and the families that will repopulate the earth, will have no trouble being pioneers of a *new world*; after all, we will be bringing people from other eras, and other worlds, that have actually been pioneers before. We will teach them, and they will rebuild," said Leo.

"This sounds very familiar to me, Leo."

"Yes indeed, said Leo. People could never figure out how the Egyptians built the pyramids, could they?"

"Will all humans perish, Leo?"

"Actually, there will be survivors. The ones that are pure in spirit will remain. Sadly, there are not enough of them to repopulate the earth, but with our help, they will rebuild, and will be rewarded for their love and caring of the human race."

Leo told Dr. Holiday that he felt that each time the world ended, the human race grew more knowledgeable, and learned by the mistakes of their ancestors; therefore, they became more highly evolved. He said that the human race would begin to realize that they could transport themselves anywhere they wanted to go, with the power of their faith. They would be able to leave their body, and return, at will. He said most of the humans that occupy the earth at this time, are so involved in ego and greed, that it is virtually impossible for them to understand why they are really here.

"Enough for now, my friend, let's go and see what Molly is making for lunch."

Chapter Five

"Ruby," asked Hannah," have you seen my dad?" "Yes, sweetheart, I believe he is having lunch with Leo on the beach deck. They should be just about done."

As Hannah and Josh walked out onto the beach deck, they caught the tail end of what Leo was saying.

"Leo," said Hannah, "I know my dad is going to be involved in training the doctors that are left behind on earth, because our techniques are much more advanced than those of the doctors on earth, I just didn't realize that he would be going to the *new world* to train these doctors."

"Don't worry, my darling," said Dr. Holiday, "I will be training on the island until there are enough doctors that can handle medical care on earth. At that time, I will start the first medical school on earth. Trust me; it won't be long until I will be back on the island with you.

"I'm sorry, Leo," said Hannah. "It's just that I love my dad so much. My brothers say I am much too protective of him, but I just can't help it. Even though we will be going with him on this expedition, I am still a little apprehensive, after all, he *is* the oldest one going on this mission."

"And probably the most capable," said Leo, "not to mention that he is the head of the medical team, even though the team consists of only two; you and your father."

"I know this, Leo, I am just so afraid of losing him. I just want him to live long enough to know his grandchildren. Can you promise me that this will happen?"

"Hannah, let's just say that your father is part of the long term plan for the *new world*. He is much too important to the new human race, for anything to happen to him."

"There will be a time, as you well know, when humans will be able to project themselves, within minutes, to any place they wish to be. There will be no death, only a time to shed your earthly body, and transcend to the next level, but until that time, you and your father will be the only doctors on this island. Even though everyone on the island is protected from the earthly elements, and diseases, many of the people coming to the island will already have medical problems that need to be treated, and you and your father have already dealt with minor problems caused from accidents. The children have not come into their powers yet, and the humans that live here now, as well as the ones that will be arriving here, will need medical attention for quite a while. This transformation will not happen overnight, and again, it will not happen to everyone at the same time. So you see how important you and your father are to this island, don't you, my dear?"

"Yes, I do understand, Leo, thank you," she said as she kissed his cheek. "I do feel so much better now, though I did get a little shock when I kissed your cheek."

Leo just smiled and said he would see everyone later for dinner.

Hannah couldn't help but think that there was so much more to Leo than anyone would ever know. She felt as if she had been charged with energy, and that it came directly from Leo. *She made a mental note to ask her father how much he really knew about Leo.*

Chapter Six

As Nicholas and Geoffrey appeared in the village where Geoffrey's mother lived, they looked around to make sure that all seemed to be normal.

Geoffrey said he was a little nervous about seeing his mother after all these years. He wondered if she would be senile by now.

Nicholas laughed and said since women married so young, back then, she was probably no more than forty-five or fifty years old.

"Well, even so, the life she has lived has to have taken its toll."

"I agree, Geoffrey, but after Catherine and Maggie get through with her, she will be a *new* woman."

By the time Nicholas and Geoffrey reached Lady Margaret's front door, they noticed a few villagers staring at them. They quickly knocked on the door, and as the door opened, Geoffrey was staring into the eyes of his mother. He never imagined that so many childhood memories would come rushing back to him so quickly. Tears began to roll down his face, and Lady Margaret never said a word, she began to cry as well.

"Geoffrey, my son, you are alive! You are home!" As the two came together, they embraced, and Nicholas closed the door so that there would be no curiosity seekers.

"Mother, I know you have many questions to ask me, as I have many questions for you, but right now I am going to ask you to trust me, and do exactly as I say. There are some men outside that I recognize from the castle, and if I recognized them, then it will soon dawn on them, who I am. We are going to have to leave this place in a few moments, and I ask that you close your eyes, and do not open them until I tell you to."

"Geoffrey, I am so happy to see you that I will do whatever you ask."

Geoffrey then introduced his mother to Nicholas, and told her that he had saved his life. "Nicholas is like a brother to me, and I trust him with my life."

"If you trust him, Geoffrey, then so shall I. I thank you, Sir Nicholas, for bringing my son back to me."

Suddenly there was a loud knock on the door.

"Open this door," said a gruff voice. "I know you are

in there, Sir Geoffrey. We all thought you had perished, but no body was found."

Geoffrey and his mother both recognized the voice as that of Prince Andrew, and Geoffrey knew that they had only seconds to escape.

"Close your eyes, Mother," said Geoffrey, "and join hands with Nicholas and me." About that time, the men burst the door down, and just as Geoffrey had suspected, one of the men was Prince Andrew.

"How dare you take me from my parents, I was told that they were dead, and then you tried to replace my father. I know the whole story, and you will pay for the crimes you committed!"

"Okay, Geoffrey," said Nicholas. "It's time to go."

"I don't think so," said Prince Andrew. "You won't be going anywhere."

Nicholas, Geoffrey, and Lady Margaret were still holding hands.

"Close your eyes, Mother, now!"

Suddenly the three of them were gone, and when they arrived back on Paradise Island, Geoffrey opened his eyes and said that said he would give anything to see the look on Prince Andrew's face about now.

"*His* face?" asked Lady Margaret. "What does *my*

face look like? I have no idea where I am, or how I even got here."

Nicholas and Geoffrey laughed and hugged Lady Margaret at the same time. "I already love you, Lady Margaret," said Nicholas. "Now, shall we share our story with your mother Geoffrey?"

Chapter Seven

Ruby was out on the front porch looking to see if Nicholas and Geoffrey had returned. She knew that Lady Margaret would be exhausted when they arrived, and she had food and beverages ready for the three of them. She wanted to take Lady Margaret under her wing. They were close to the same age, and she knew that the younger ones could not relate to her as well as she could.

Just as she was about to go back inside, she saw three figures walking towards her. As they got near, Ruby knew that this was indeed Lady Margaret.

"Welcome back, my time travelers," said Ruby. "And you must be Lady Margaret." "Yes, I am, and you would be Ruby?"

"Indeed I am, please come into the kitchen for something cool to drink."

"Mother, Nicholas and I will be having a bath, and changing clothes. You are in very capable hands with Ruby. She will take you to your quarters, and explain all the gadgets to you. I'll join you in a while on the beach deck."

Geoffrey and Nicholas both gave her a big hug, and ran upstairs to shower.

Ruby took Lady Margaret to the kitchen, and poured them both a tall glass of iced tea. "Please, sit down Lady Margaret, I know that Nicholas and Geoffrey filled you in on what is about to take place and I'm assuming that, by now, you are completely terrified, and are trying to hide it from all of us."

"You more than likely assumed that you and Geoffrey are both dead, and that Nicholas is the Angel of death that came with Geoffrey to bring you to the great beyond. When you saw this beautiful island, you naturally felt that you must be in heaven."

"Yes and I assumed that you are one of the angels."

"So far, no one on this island has ever called me an angel, Lady Margaret. I am here because Leo asked for my help. I run the household, with the help of others that you will meet later today."

"So Leo is a real person?" Nicholas and Geoffrey told me about him and the part he played in their being here; but again, I felt that I had crossed over to the heavens."

"I am very much alive," said Leo as he walked into the kitchen. "And I am honored to meet you, Lady Margaret."

"And I am honored to meet you, also, Leo."

Leo then asked Ruby to show Lady Margaret to her

room, and since she was so kind as to offer to be her mentor, he hoped that in the next few days, they could have a welcome party for Geoffrey's mother.

"Ruby said that she intended to spend as much time with Lady Margaret as possible, in order to bring her up to date on the world as it is now. I know there will be much more for her to learn, but I believe that between Catherine, Molly, and me, Lady Margaret will be quite ready for her welcome party by tomorrow night."

Chapter Eight

Late that afternoon, Nicholas, Claire, Geoffrey, and Heather met out on the beach deck. Molly had the bar set up for cocktails and appetizers. Soon, Hannah, Josh, and Dr. Holiday joined them. They were discussing Geoffrey's mother, when Michael and Charles arrived.

"I know the two of you missed us, didn't you?" asked Michael.

"With all our heart," said Nicholas.

"So, where's your Mum?" asked Charles.

"Ruby has her hidden away, so that you two don't scare her half to death."

"I know this is hard for you to believe, Geoffrey, but Charles and I promised each other we would not make any snide remarks to you until your mother has had a chance to know us."

"Otherwise, she may try and run us through for teasing her baby boy," said Charles.

"You two cannot rattle me today, I have my mother back, I have my soul mate beside me, I have Nicholas and Claire, who have become my brother and sister, and I have Leo, who is like a father to me."

"So, what are we to you, Geoffrey?" asked Michael. "You two are like brothers also, but more like little brothers that pester the daylights out of you. You get on my nerves, but I love ya anyway."

"That was lovely," said Leo, as he walked out onto the deck. "Geoffrey, your mother will be with Ruby until tomorrow night. I believe that Ruby will be able to ready her for our way of life faster than anyone on this island. She assures me that your mother will be ready for a welcome party by tomorrow night; and knowing Ruby, I believe it; however, Lady Margaret did request that you come and bid her goodnight."

"I thank you, Leo; not only for what you have given me, but for bringing my mother to the island. I assure you that my loyalty lies with you forever."

"Say goodnight to your mother for me, my son."

"And for me as well," said Nicholas.

Chapter Nine

As Geoffrey rapped lightly on the door to his mother's room, he felt as if he were a little boy again. He remembered his mother always kissing him goodnight, and telling him that he was a very special being. She used to say that no matter what happened in his life, and no matter where he was, they would always end up back together.

Ruby opened the door, and said that she and Lady Margaret had quite an afternoon together. She said that his mother was a quick study. They went through indoor plumbing and air conditioning. They had an early dinner brought up to them, and now it was time for his mother to rest.

As Geoffrey entered the room, and saw his mother looking out the window at the beach, he knew that the two of them had much in common.

"Mother, I just wanted to say goodnight, and that I am so happy to have you back in my life."

"Geoffrey, my son, I have no idea why, but I have always known that you and I would be together again. I love you more than you will ever know."

"I love you as well; Mother and I will see you in the morning."

Geoffrey," said Ruby, "I would like for you to join your mother for breakfast in the morning. I am having a very special breakfast sent up to the two of you, but after breakfast, I will have her for the rest of the day; that is, until dinner tomorrow night."

"That sounds perfect, Ruby."

As Geoffrey kissed his mother goodnight, he whispered that he felt that all was right in his world. He also hugged Ruby, and said that he could never repay her for taking care of his mother.

"You already have, Geoffrey, have a wonderful evening."

"Geoffrey," said Lady Margaret, "I feel that I am in a dream from which I cannot awaken, not that I want to if it meant never seeing my son again."

"I know, Mother. When I first arrived, I thought I was in Heaven, and I can tell you that it is as close to Heaven as I've ever been."

"Between what you, Nicholas and Ruby have told me, I realize that we are in the twenty first century, so I understand that there would be much progress made, I am just overwhelmed with how much has been made. I do not understand very much of anything, at this time, I am just grateful to finally have you back with me."

Geoffrey had already explained to his mother, immediately after they arrived on the island, that he knew the story about her and the prince, and how she was actually Lady Margaret, of the Castle of King Arthur. In fact, he told her everything that he knew or remembered about his past.

"Now I am anxious to hear about the parts of my childhood that I don't remember, but that can wait till morning. You need your rest, and I am sure you will sleep like a baby tonight. We will continue this conversation in the morning. I love you, Mother, and I am so happy that we are finally together."

"As am I, my son, and I love you as well."

Geoffrey took his time joining the others on the beach deck, because he wanted to have a little time to himself. He walked out onto the front porch, sat in one of the rockers, and silently

said a prayer of thanks that he had been reunited with his mother, and he also prayed that his father was someplace as wonderful as The Island of Bliss.

Chapter Ten

"Excuse me everyone," said Heather, "I will be right back."
For some reason, Heather went straight to the front porch.

"I hope I'm not disturbing you, my love," said Heather.

"You could never disturb me," said Geoffrey. "In fact, I was just thinking about you, so you must have heard me. I left my mother a while ago, and I still find it hard to believe that I have her back. It's like a dream." I am so happy that she is here, but I'm afraid that when I wake in the morning, she will be gone." "You know that Leo would never allow something so cruel to happen to anyone as long as they reside on this island," said Heather.

"She will not be gone, my darling, I promise you. Now, unless you would like a little more time to yourself, Nicholas, Claire and I waited to have dinner with you."

Geoffrey laughed and said, "My dear, have you ever seen me turn down a wonderful meal? Especially with my bride-to-be and the best friends I have ever had."

Nicholas and Claire were waiting on the deck for Geoffrey and Heather, when they noticed that the sky looked rather strange. They knew that this was not a storm, but neither one had ever seen anything like it.

"We should ask my father about this tomorrow," said Claire.

"Ask your father about what?" asked Geoffrey, as he and Heather arrived on the beach deck.

"The sky," said Claire. "Nicholas and I were wondering what could be happening. We have neither one seen anything like it."

Geoffrey and Heather agreed that neither of them had ever seen anything like it, and that Leo probably was the only one that could tell them what was going on.

Claire and Heather went to the kitchen to bring the food out that Molly prepared for the four of them, and when they returned, they said that they all needed to get some sleep tonight, because tomorrow was going to be wild.

Claire and Heather's parents were arriving, the parents of the orphans were arriving, and Nicholas and Geoffrey had to start preparing for their Santa gig.

"We probably won't be seeing much of each other for the next few days," said Heather. "Claire and I will be tied up with my mother, and Claire's two mothers, making wedding plans. Catherine and Maggie will be assisting the Grays with the introduction of the children to their parents."

"Where will they be staying?" asked Geoffrey.

"Father said they will be staying in the bungalows on the beach," said Claire. "The Grays, as well as Catherine and Maggie, will be living close by, in order to make sure all goes well. It shouldn't be too hard for the parents to adjust; after all, they came from another planet, not another lifetime. The meetings will be more emotional than anything, and Heather and I decided the children needed to bond with their parents for a few days before we introduce ourselves."

Chapter Eleven

The next few weeks were filled with preparations or parties of one kind or another. First, there was Lady Margaret's welcome party, then a welcome party for the parents of the orphans. A tree trimming party, and the next party was to be for the parents of the brides and grooms.

"Father," asked Claire, as she caught up with Leo walking toward the beach, "may I have a few moments of your time?"

"You may have all the time you want, my sweetheart,"

"Thank you, Father; it's just that there are a couple of things I would like to ask you."

"Go right ahead, my dear."

"Well, remember when Nicholas and I asked you about the strange sky a couple of weeks ago?"

"Yes, I remember."

"Well, you said it was a part of many strange things that would take place before the end of the world."

"That's right, Claire, I did say that."

. "Well last night, I couldn't sleep, so I took a walk to

the beach, and I saw something that was strange to me, yet somehow familiar. I saw so many spacecrafts in the sky, and though I don't remember ever seeing one, it felt as if I had actually been inside one of them."

"That's because you have, Claire. You know you were not born here, and though you were quite small, we brought you here in one of those very same spacecrafts."

"But how do you know that these are the same ones, Father?"

. "Because I ordered them here, they are going to be circling the earth for a few days, and will be reporting back to me, if there are any changes that I need to know about."

"Like what, Father?"

"Claire, you know we intend to rescue the humans that are pure in spirit, and bring them to the island before the end, but what I didn't tell you is that it looks as if the end may be sooner than we thought."

"Why, Father?"

"Because a horrid entity has immerged, that we thought had been destroyed many years ago and he wants the earth for himself, and his followers, and he is trying to do everything in his power to cause the earth to end sooner than we had anticipated. By doing this, he thinks he can gain control over it before we know what is happening, but what he doesn't know is that I have our people watching him, and we are onto his plans. We may not be able to stop what he has put into motion, but we can slow him down, until we are able to find him and his followers, and put an end to them once and for all. There will simply be no evil."

"I trust you, Father, but I am still a little frightened."

"I don't want you to be frightened, Claire; you are safe as long as you are on this island."

"That is reassuring."

"Oh, I forgot that I had something else to ask you; Geoffrey, Hannah, and I, all have parents that will be at the wedding, but Nicholas has no one. I know he is like a son to you, Father, but does he not have family anywhere that could be here?"

"My Sweetheart, I do have a very big surprise for Nicholas, before the wedding, but I don't want you to mention this to him. He needs to concentrate on the children for Christmas, and you must concentrate on the wedding."

"Well may I at least tell him what you told me about the space craft in the sky?"

"He already knows, my dear."

Chapter Twelve

It was now a week and a half before Christmas, and the island was filled with wonder. The whole island was alive with lights. The wedding was to take place in the enchanted forest, and the reception would be at the main house. Nicholas and Geoffrey were totally ready to deliver gifts Christmas Eve, and Leo and Ciara had made plans for the two couples to have a honeymoon on a part of the island that none of them had even seen.

The day before the weddings, Nicholas felt the urge to have some time alone, so he decided to take a drive to the aquarium. It was a wonderful place to meditate, or just sit, relax, and watch the underwater creatures. As Nicholas walked into the aquarium, he felt a calmness come over him; a calmness like he had never felt before. It was as if time had suddenly stood still.

After choosing a big overstuffed chair, Nicholas sat down, relaxed and began to watch all the beautiful sea creatures and before long, he felt as if he were drifting away.

The next time he opened his eyes, his father and mother were standing before him.

"Father, Mother? I must be dreaming."

"No, son," said his father. "You are not dreaming. We are here with you, but only for a while. We are helping with the plans to rebuild the earth; in fact, I knew about this when you were just a young boy. You see, your mother and I are not from this planet, and like many others, we have been monitoring Earth for many years."

"There is so much more to be done, my son, but it can wait until after the wedding, right now your mother and I want nothing more than to be with you."

As Nicholas stood up and walked toward his mother and father, he couldn't believe they were really here, but as he reached out to them, they both wrapped their arms around him, and said that someday soon, they would also be living on the island, and would never have to leave again.

"I can't tell you how happy that makes me; I have missed you both so much."

"And we have missed you more than you will ever know, my son," said Nicholas's mother, "your father and I just need some time alone with our son."

"I would love nothing more, Mother, but I don't think we will have any time alone tonight. There is a dinner planned for the family of the bride and groom."

"Well, at least we will be able to see your beautiful bride," said Nicholas's father. "My goodness, we haven't seen her since she was a little girl, living on this island."

"You know her?"

"Yes, son, but we will discuss that later; right now, I suggest we get a move on, don't want to miss the big dinner."

As they drove to the main house, Nicholas felt as if his life would always be one surprise after another. *Thank God this surprise was a good one*, he thought.

Chapter Thirteen

"Ayden, Deidre," said Leo, as Nicholas and his parents walked up the stairs to the front porch of the main house. "We are so happy you were able to make it for the wedding."

"You knew they were coming, didn't you, Leo?" asked Nicholas. "That's why you're standing out here; you were waiting for me to bring them back."

Ciara walked out about that time, hugged her old friends, and welcomed them back.

Leo told Nicholas that Claire was so concerned that he had no real family attending the wedding, that, he almost broke down and told her, but he was afraid that she would not be able to keep it from him, so he decided to surprise both of them.

"So what do you all say to joining the bride-to-be on the waterfall deck for cocktails before dinner?" asked Leo.

"I for one say yes, yes, and yes," said Ayden, as he put his arm around Leo's shoulder. "Being with our family and friends, is just what we all need tonight."

Geoffrey, Heather and Claire were waiting for

Nicholas to meet them on the Waterfall deck, and Claire was about to tell them how badly she felt for Nicholas, since he would be the only one without a parent at the wedding, when Nicholas and the others showed up

"Claire, you won't believe what happened, my parents are here.

Mother, Father, I would like you to meet my beautiful, Claire. Actually, you already know Claire, don't you?"

"Darling," said Deirdre, "that was many years ago. Claire was much too young to remember us, but you are right, she is quite beautiful."

After all the introductions were made, Nicholas told Claire what had happened that afternoon, and that he never knew that his parents were involved in what would be transpiring in the *new world*. He said that there were many things that he never knew about his parents, and they all began to laugh.

"We never meant to keep you in the dark, Nicholas," said Ayden, "but when Leo contacted us and said that it was time for you to come to the island, we were relieved. We knew we would have to leave soon, and we couldn't take you with us, yet we couldn't tell you what was about to happen. You were not to know anything until you arrived on the island."

By this time, Geoffrey's mother and Heather's parents

had arrived, and not long after came Claire's other parents, and her sister Adrian.

After Leo toasted the brides and grooms and their families, they all went inside for their family dinner. Everyone had a wonderful evening catching up and spending time with their families.

Cameron and Lauren, the aunt and uncle that raised Claire, said that they loved Claire as if she were their own, and Adrian said that as far as she was concerned, Claire was, and always would be her sister.

"By the way," asked Adrian, "since you and Dad are not from the planet earth, does this mean I'm an alien also?"

Everyone laughed as Lauren said they always thought she was an alien.

" But seriously, my dear, though you were born on earth, you are the child of aliens, so yes, you are an alien, so to speak, However; this is a good thing, my sweetie, soon you will come into your own powers."

"Cool, so I guess that means Heather will also have powers since you and Uncle Jeremy are brothers."

Heather's parents, Jeremy and Leann started laughing.

"Heather will indeed have powers, very soon," said Jeremy, "but somehow I don't think she feels it's that *cool*.

Maybe you could get her to loosen up a little, and realize that it is just a part of who she is."

"No problem, Uncle Jeremy," said Adrian. "You and Aunt Leann can just relax, and I'll take care of Heather."

"I'm sure that makes Aunt Leann feel much better, dear," said Lauren, as she smiled and winked at Leann.

Chapter Fourteen

The next day, all seemed to be going according to schedule, when suddenly the skies became very dark. Leo had already warned everyone that the end of the world was near, and there would be many more signs before this took place. He told everyone that as long as they were on the island, there was nothing to worry about, and those that were to remain on earth, would be taken care of.

The wedding was quite beautiful, and, of course, Leo officiated. Claire and Heather made sure that all the children were part of the wedding party, and having the ceremony in the Enchanted Forest proved to be the most suitable place on the island. The trees and wildflowers were the perfect decorations, and sounds of the small creatures in the forest provided such relaxing sounds, that it was almost mesmerizing.

As soon as everyone arrived back at the main house, Charles and Michael said that this was going to be their favorite part of the whole wedding.

Leo said that if the truth were known, Geoffrey would probably agree.

"Where is Geoffrey anyway?" asked Lady Margaret.

"Oh, I believe they are changing into clothes more suitable for the reception," said Mr. Lovejoy. "By the way, Lady Margaret, thank you for allowing me to escort you to the wedding."

My pleasure, Mr. Lovejoy, and you may call me Margaret."

"Very well, Margaret, if you agree to call me Lionel."

Yes, Lionel, I do agree."

"Something tells me that there is a romance brewing between those two," said Hannah. "You are usually right about these things," said Josh. "But don't let Geoffrey hear you say that."

"Don't let Geoffrey hear you say what?" asked Geoffrey, as he walked out onto the beach deck.

"She said that she loved those little crabmeat appetizers so much," said Josh. "that she might just eat them all herself, but I was in the process of reminding her that you love them as much as she does, so she had better not tell you about her plan."

"That is true, I do love them but I am so happy today that I am willing to share them with you Miss Hannah."

"I would have saved you some anyway Geoffrey."

"I'm sure glad we decided on an island theme for our reception, Mrs. Christopher," said Nicholas, as he and Claire came out to the beach deck.

"As am I, Mr. Christopher," said Claire.

"But I am really excited about our honeymoon; an entire week of being alone with my very own Santa Claus."

Watch it, Mrs. Claus," said Nicholas, "or I'll have you baking cookies for the entire island."

Nicholas and Geoffrey told Charles and Michael that this was the best party they had ever been to on the island.

"Wouldn't have anything to do with the fact that it was in *your* honor, would it?" said Michael.

"Of course not," said Geoffrey. "Nicholas and I are quite humble men, ya know, Mikie. We don't need the limelight; we shine with no help from the likes of you two."

"Be nice, Geoff," said Nicholas. "They did put this whole party together for us, you know."

"I know, Nickie but if I were to let my guard down around theses two, can you imagine how badly they would persecute me?"

"Persecute is a pretty harsh word, Sir Geoffrey," said Charles. "We only harass you because we like you so much; and to prove it, we have written a toast to you and Nicholas."

"I'm really afraid of this one," said Geoffrey.

"Don't worry Geoffrey; they know they cannot go very far when Leo is around."

"Quiet everyone," said Michael. "Charles and I have written a toast to Nicholas and Geoffrey, on their wedding day, a day they will never forget."

"Why does that sound like a threat to me, Nickie?"

. "Relax, Geoff, they are just trying to intimidate you,"

"Well it's working."

"Ladies and Gentlemen, Michael and I would like to make a toast to Nicholas and Geoffrey."

"The words kind, loving, brave, and compassionate, describe these two. From the first time we met them, we knew that we would be great friends; little did we know that we would become more like brothers. To Nicholas and Geoffrey, We love you guys."

"Ditto!" said Geoffrey.

"Okay, Chuckie," said Michael, "enough of the sappy stuff. I have a toast of my own. Nickie, Geoffrey, remember when we had our first cook out for the two of you? We all wore our flowered shirts, our shorts and flip-flops, and the four of us bonded to a particular song. Well, don't worry guys, I'm not going to ask you to sing it, as a matter of fact, I'm gonna sing it for you, myself."

Nicholas and Geoffrey were both shocked when Michael got on the stage that had been constructed on the beach deck. He grabbed a microphone, and when the music began to play, Michael began to sing, *"I Love this Bar."*

Needless to say, everyone loved it, and requested an encore.

As everyone danced, Nicholas told Claire that never in his life would he have ever imagined that he would end up in Paradise with the most beautiful female in the universe.

"My goodness, I did hit the jackpot when I married you, didn't I Nicholas?"

Nicholas just smiled and said that he hoped she always felt that way.

Chapter Fifteen

After the two couples left for their honeymoon, on the other side of the island, Leo summoned Doctor Holiday.

"Zach, my friend, I must ask a big favor of you."

"Of course, Leo, you know I will do whatever you ask of me."

"I know that, Zach, but it seems that all is not going exactly as we had anticipated. It seems that the end is nearing much sooner than we thought, so I must ask that you and your group leave the island immediately after the Christmas holiday. I didn't say anything to Nicholas and Geoffrey, because I didn't want them to worry about this while they are on their honeymoon. I'm afraid they will have to leave at the same time that you do."

"What has happened to cause this, Leo?"

"I would say that Mother Nature has just had quite enough, and she seems to be trying to right all the wrongs that have been done to the planet. Let's just say that her patience ran out a little sooner than expected."

"So how much time will we have once we leave the island?"

"No more than two weeks, if that."

"Two weeks? We need two months to accomplish all that we need to do before we return to the island."

"I am aware of that, my friend; that is why I said it was a huge favor. I would not think less of you if you decided to stay on the island; this is a lot to ask of you and the others."

"But I would think less of me, Leo. I know you would go if it were possible for you to leave the island."

"Indeed," said Leo, "however, I must warn you that aside from having less time to accomplish all that needs to be accomplished, you will also be dealing with some humans that will not make it easy for you. As you know, there is a select group of scientists, doctors, and teachers that will be waiting for you when you arrive. But what I have recently found out, is that there is also a group of world leaders that not only know that the destruction of their planet is near, they have also found out that there is a rescue team coming for those that have been chosen to rebuild the earth. Needless to say, these leaders are not pure in spirit, and they will do whatever it takes to infiltrate the group of the chosen ones."

"How did they find out about the mission, Leo, I cannot imagine anyone leaking this information."

"It wasn't leaked by our group Zach. You see, there was a man that I called my friend. In the beginning, he was a very important part of the plan, but he let his ego overtake his spirit. He felt that, with what he knew, he could take control of the island, and with the help of some of his confidantes on earth, he could rule the *new world*. I was told that he died, but it was just a trick to throw us off. By the time I realized that he was still alive, he put together his own army so he could control the people that would repopulate the earth. He knows that the end is near, and he also knows that he must bring his army to the island in order to be saved, so he is on the lookout for our team because he knows that we they will be returning to the island, and he intends to return with them. What he doesn't know is that even if he made it to the island, he could not step one foot on it, because of his intentions. The island would not allow it, however, we can't afford to let him get anywhere near our team because as soon as you leave the island, you become very vulnerable. . He does expect aircraft and possibly spacecraft to be the means of transportation back to the island so I have chosen another mode of transportation for you all. We will meet again when Nicholas returns, my friend. In the meantime, let's enjoy the rest of this party."

Chapter Sixteen

As soon as Nicholas, Claire, Geoffrey, and Heather returned from the honeymoon, they were greeted by Leo. He welcomed them back, and said that all the adults, with the exception of Catherine and Maggie, would be dinning together this evening. He said that Catherine and Maggie would be attending to the young ones so that the adults would be able to talk openly about the events that would be taking place after the holiday.

After dinner, Leo announced the rescue plan had been moved up.

"I really don't want to go into a lot of detail but I have made a decision to accelerate the rescue plan. There is much less time left for earth than anticipated."

"There will also be very little time for the Grays, as well as Mr. Lovejoy, Ms Pierce, and Capt. Stokes to view Planet Earth as it is in the 21st century. Fortunately, Nicholas and Geoffrey have left the island a few times, and have seen the progress that has been made. The rest of you will at least be able to see some of the earth's most important landmarks."

"You will be flying to New York City, the day after Christmas, and will have the privilege of seeing the Statue of Liberty, in person. The rest of your itinerary will be given to you upon departure of the island. If you have any questions, feel free to ask, otherwise, have a wonderful evening."

As Leo left the dinning room, you could hear a pin drop. Seeing that everyone was dumbfounded, Nicholas stood up and told everyone they were all chosen for this mission by Leo, and that in itself was an honor.

"If it had not been for Leo, not one of us would be here right now. We owe our allegiance not only to Leo, but also to our children on the island, and to their children, the future children of Planet Earth. We are all the chosen ones, and we will be the first generation to understand what it is like to live without limits. We will be the first to be able to transport our souls throughout the universe, without dying first."

"I cannot speak for the rest of you but I, myself, feel extremely honored to be chosen to be one of the pilgrims of the *new world*. To be able to teach the children that love is all there is, and that the more love we have in our hearts, the higher our souls will soar, and there will be no distinction between Heaven and earth."

Everyone stood and smiled with pride at what Nicholas said. As each person left the room, they touched

Nicholas in a way that let him know that they were all proud to be part of the *New Beginning*.

After everyone was gone, Nicholas asked Claire if she and Heather minded if he and Geoffrey had a little time alone together.

Claire and Heather both said that they were very tired anyway, and would see the two of them later.

After the ladies left, Nicholas poured him and Geoffrey a glass of Brandy, and they walked out onto the beach deck. Nicholas raised his glass and said, "Heaven be with both of us, Geoffrey."

As Geoffrey raised his glass to toast Nicholas, he said that as much as he was looking forward to his first Christmas, he was not in a big hurry for it to come, since they would be leaving the island the day after.

"Under different circumstances it would be something to look forward to," said Nicholas, "seeing planet earth in this century."

"Yes, it would be great fun if we could just be tourists," said Geoffrey, "but I have a feeling that there won't be a lot of time for sightseeing."

Nicholas didn't tell Geoffrey that Leo wanted to meet with him alone after breakfast the next day. He had a feeling that what he had to discuss with him was not pleasant.

"By the way," asked Geoffrey, "what did you want

to speak with me about? You did tell the ladies that you wanted a word with me."

"Oh yes, I almost forgot. You know we move to our new homes tomorrow, and we have a lot to do so that the children will have a good Christmas, so I just thought it might be nice for the two of us to have a little Nicholas and Geoffrey time before all the madness begins."

Chapter Seventeen

The next Morning Doctor Holiday joined Leo for an early breakfast.

"Good morning, my friend," said Leo, as the Doctor approached.

"And a very good morning to you, Leo. I see we are the only ones up this early and, in fact, I am glad we are alone."

"And I think I know why," said Leo. "You heard me say that the team would be going to

New York yet I told you that the ones watching for us would be expecting us to use aircraft as transportation, however; you will be using other means of transportation that I cannot disclose at this time."

"Oh and before I forget, Here is a list of people that you will need to keep your eyes open for. I am giving it to you because you will recognize many of them from your visits to The White House. Some of these names are of people you knew quite well, but are definitely not our friends."

Just then, Nicholas walked in, and Leo invited him to join them for breakfast.

"I would love to Leo; Claire, Heather and Geoffrey are having breakfast with the children. I told them that I was on a mission this morning, and that you never ask questions around Christmas time."

"By the way, where is Ciara this morning?"

"Well, my boy, Ciara and her sister are out for an early morning walk on the beach, and then they plan to spend the rest of the day decorating for Christmas."

"And speaking of Christmas," said Doctor Holiday, "I have some secrets of my own to take care of. I hope to see you all for dinner this evening."

After the Doctor left, Leo told Nicholas that he wanted to make sure that he keep this conversation to himself. "No one, not even Claire is to know what I am about to tell you."

"Leo you know that I am completely loyal to you, and I also know that if you have something to tell me that cannot be repeated to my wife, your daughter, then it must be for her good as well as the others."

"Yes, Nicholas, it is indeed in the best interest for everyone.

Leo then went on to tell him about the enemies that would be watching for them. He told him that Doctor Holiday knew some of these men from his many visits to earth from his planet, and would be able to recognize them, so he did tell him who these men were.

"I also told him that you would be flying into New York; what I didn't tell him is that you will be *sailing out*."

"I don't understand, Sir."

"These men that want to rule the world will be expecting us to bring everyone back to the island by aircraft so I want no one to know how I intend to transport you all back, no one except you that is."

"On the day you depart New York, you will be leading your team to the place of your departure. I am about to give you your instructions, and I want them committed to memory. This is of the utmost importance, Nicholas. We can't afford to put anything in writing."

After Leo left, Nicholas decided to take a walk on the beach and go over everything Leo had told him. He knew that there was no room for error in this plan, and that everyone would be counting on him to bring them home safely. He was very proud that Leo thought so highly of him, yet he was also a little overwhelmed. He knew that of all the missions he had gone on so far, this was the most dangerous one of all. He would be responsible for so many lives, and the future of the *new world* hinged on how successful this mission really was. This in itself was enough to make Nicholas cringe.

Chapter Eighteen

The next few weeks seemed to fly by for everyone one the island because there were so many things going on at one time. The children were getting to know their parents, Nicholas and Geoffrey were getting a taste of how it feels to run Santa's workshop, Claire and Heather were busy helping their mothers plan the big Christmas Eve party, and everyone was helping with the decorating.

Leo was standing on the beach deck, watching all the hustle and bustle going on, and thinking about what a special Christmas this would be.

Everyone on the island had become one big family that loved each other very much, and soon this family would begin to grow, and spread throughout the New World. At least this was the plan, but Leo also knew that once the team left the island, there was no guarantee that they would be safe. Yes, they were pure in spirit, and Nicholas was indeed the chosen one, but there was never a guarantee that he would be able to complete his mission, and live; after all many men had sacrificed their lives for their Gods and their countries.

One thing Leo did know for sure is that even if Nicholas or any other members of this special team lost their lives, they would all be reunited again in the future.

Leo also knew that it would be many years before every soul in the universe understood that they are a soul with a body, instead of a body with a soul, but he also knew that when each

and every one of them experienced their own awakening; they would then know the meaning of Heaven.

"You certainly are in deep thought, Sir," said Geoffrey. And as Leo turned quickly to see Geoffrey standing there, he actually seemed startled.

"Well, Sir Leo, this is certainly one for the books. I can now actually say that I finally got to sneak up on you."

Leo burst into laughter and said that not only did Geoffrey sneak up on him and surprise him, but that he was actually the first one on the island to do this.

"Oh, don't worry, Sir, I won't tell anyone."

"Of course you will, my boy; after all, this just proves that you are becoming more and more enlightened,"

"Or that you were very deep in thought about those of us that will be going on the mission," said Geoffrey. "I think I will let this one slide."

"I have to say that you have really picked up the modern day slang rather quickly, Geoffrey."

"Thank you Sir; kind of makes me feel that I fit in with the younger generation."

"I understand what you are saying, Geoffrey. By the way, I have a question for you."

"What question, Sir?"

"Geoffrey, I know you have wondered why I brought your mother back here, and not your father, and I also know you were afraid to ask because you might not want to hear the answer.

Geoffrey, my son, your father is very much pure in spirit, but there are reasons that he cannot be with us at this time. I promise that you will understand someday."

"Thank you, Sir, that is a great relief for me, and I'm sure it will be for my mother, as well, that is if she ever accepts that she is not yet in heaven."

Chapter Nineteen

Christmas Eve arrived greeting everyone on the island with the most magical snowfall anyone had ever seen. The snowflakes took on the appearance of multicolored glitter because the island was lit up with thousands of Christmas lights.

The children were treated to a sleigh ride to Santa's Workshop because suddenly there were horses on the island.

A few days earlier, Leo told Nicholas that there was now a small horse ranch on the island, and that the Grays were taking care of the horses since they knew so much about them.

He also said that each child would be given his or her own horse as a Christmas present, but they would also be responsible for its care.

As he listened to Leo, Nicholas couldn't help but wonder just how big this island was.

"When you return from your mission, Nicholas, I will personally take you on a tour of Paradise Island; you will find that it is much larger than have imagined."

Nicholas just smiled and made a mental note to be very careful of his thoughts around Leo.

As Claire and Heather gave the children a tour of the workshop, Nicholas and Geoffrey were delivering Christmas gifts to the main house. The children would all gather at the main house after the tour, for a Christmas Eve celebration, and would exchange gifts that each of them had made with the help of Santa's helpers, of course.

After the party was over, the children would return to their own homes, and once they were asleep, Nicholas and Geoffrey would deliver the gifts from Santa.

"Merry Christmas everyone," said Leo, as all the children and their parents poured into the main house. "I hope you are all ready for your very first Christmas on the Island of Bliss." Of course, all the children were so exhilarated, that they seemed to be floating three feet off the floor.

"You know, Father," said Claire, "even though I remember the paper mache Christmas ball, I don't remember Christmas on the island."

"That's because you were so young when you left the island. Your mother and I had never celebrated Christmas ourselves, but over the years, we found it to be one of the traditions of humans that we truly wanted to share with souls from the entire universe.

The legend of Santa Claus really is so much fun for the children; of all ages might I add, but it is also one of the most spiritual celebrations on earth. Even though not everyone has the same religious beliefs, those that are pure in spirit believe in the spirit of Christmas."

"And speaking of the Christmas spirit," said Claire, "I would like to make a toast to the parents that introduced Christmas to me, and nurtured me, as if I were their very own child, and gave me the most wonderful sister that anyone could ever ask for. *To my Mom and Dad, Cameron and Lauren, I love you.*"

As everyone lifted their glasses and toasted, Claire said,

"I'm not through, yet, everyone. I *do* have another set of parents, you know. Though I didn't get to know my biological parents very well until I came to the island, I can only imagine the love they must have had for me to be able to part with me in order to protect me. We may have lost many years together, but the love we have shared since we reunited has made me realize that it's not the amount of time that you spend with someone you love that matters; it's what you do with that time; therefore, this second toast is to my original parents, Leo and Ciera. *Thank you for loving me enough to let me go and for allowing me to finally know you, and feel all the love you held in your heart for me, for all those years.*"

Chapter Twenty

"Listen up everyone," said Nicholas. *"There will be plenty of time for the rest of us to* toast one another, later on in the evening, but for now, what do you say to getting this gift giving thing started. We have a magnificent Christmas tree, loaded with presents, a huge roaring fire, and best of all; as I'm sure Geoffrey would agree, the most delectable looking appetizers that I for one have ever seen; besides, these children do need to get to sleep at a decent hour so that Santa Claus doesn't have to stay up all night."

Everyone agreed that having the children exchange gifts with each other would be a wonderful way to start their first Christmas celebration together. They would each celebrate Christmas with their families in the morning, and meet again at the main house for Christmas dinner.

There were not that many children on the island yet, so the gift exchanging didn't take very long, but the most unexpected, as well as touching part of the evening was when the children, as a group, presented Leo and Ciara,

Claire and Heather, and Nicholas and Geoffrey, each a certificate of their love and appreciation.

Leo and Ciera's certificate was for making it possible for them to be reunited with their parents again. Claire and Heather's certificate was for loving them for all the years that they were without their parents, and Nicholas and Geoffrey, for teaching them so many things that a father would have taught them since they came to the island.

Leo read *The Night Before Christmas* to the children, and afterwards all the families left the main house to return to their own homes and wait for Santa Claus. Everyone, that is, except the Gray family.

"Is there something wrong?" asked Nicholas.

"Not really, Nicholas," said Amelia. "It's just that Joseph and I wanted to give you and Geoffrey something we made, but we wanted to give it to you in private."

"Why?" asked Geoffrey. "Is it something the other children might try and take from us?"

"No," said Amelia, giggling. "It's just that our gift meant something different than theirs."

"Yeah," said Joseph, "you rescued our whole family, and made us a part of your family. We all feel like you are the uncles we never had, so if it's alright with you, we made official adoption papers."

"Joseph, Amelia," said Nicholas, "I cannot think of a

more thoughtful Christmas gift than this one, because it is the gift of your love."

"You already know how I feel about the two of ya," said Geoffrey. "I'm just honored that you feel the same way about me."

"So does that mean we can call you Uncle Nicholas and Uncle Geoffrey?" asked Amelia.

"Hey, its official isn't it?" said Nicholas, "after all, you have the papers to prove it."

"Oh, they're official alright," said Jacob. "They were signed by Leo himself, and they even have a gold seal."

"There is a copy for both our families," said Amelia. "Welcome to our family."

"And welcome to ours," said Nicholas, as he and Geoffrey exchanged hugs with the entire Gray family.

"Ditto," said Geoffrey, as they walked the Grays out, "and to all, a good night."

Nicholas and Geoffrey watched the Grays as they headed toward their own home, and Geoffrey said that he wished he had thought of getting Leo to sign a paper saying that he and Nicholas were brothers.

"Geoffrey, you are my brother, and I don't need a piece of paper to make it official. In fact, we could make it official ourselves."

"How can we do that Nicholas?"

"We can start our own family tradition. When we

get the sleigh loaded with the gifts for the children, we can make a special toast to each other, and every year, we will make the same toast. How does that sound?"

"Sounds great, Nickie, Just tell me what to say, and I'll say it."

"No, Geoff, you have to make up your own toast. It has to come from your heart. Just think about it while we are loading the sleigh. Think about what it is about me that makes you think of me as a brother, and a friend."

Chapter Twenty One

"Okay you two" said Heather, *"It's time that the four of us head back to the North* Pole."

"Hey Nick, do ya think we will ever actually see the real North Pole?" asked Geoffrey, as they followed Heather back inside the house.

"I really hope not, Geoffrey, from what I understand, no one in their right mind ever goes there, on purpose."

Leo and Ciara were waiting for Nicholas and Geoffrey when they came back into the main house.

"Nicholas, Geoffrey," said Leo, "we are not going to hold the four of you up any longer. You have a long, yet wonderful night ahead of you. Tomorrow is Christmas day. We will start the day with a Christmas brunch with our immediate family, and afterwards we can exchange our gifts. In the meantime, have a magical night, and know that you are loved."

"By everyone on this island," said Ciara, as she raised her glass to toast the four.

Lady Margaret, Geoffrey's mother, Claire's other parents, Cameron and Lauren, Heather's parents, Leann and Jeremy, and Nicholas's parents, Deirdre and Ayden raised their glasses as well. "*Here, Here,*" they all said.

As the four headed back to the workshop to load the gifts on the sleigh, they could hear voices saying, *"Merry Christmas, we love you."* And they knew that this would indeed be the most memorable Christmas any of them had ever had.

By the time the four arrived at the workshop, the helpers had already loaded the sleigh. There was a note on door saying that there was a list in the sleigh stating which gifts went to which child. They said that they had to return to their own planet, for their own celebration, but that they hoped to see them again very soon.

"Guess Christmas must have rubbed off on them," said Geoffrey.

"How do you know that they didn't already have Christmas before the people on earth?" asked Heather.

Claire said that she for one hoped that Christmas was celebrated throughout the universe.

"I hope so as well Claire" said Nicholas "Though we do know one thing for sure."

"What's that Nicholas?"

"There has never been, nor will there ever be, a Santa anywhere to compare with Geoffrey and me; however, if we do not get going, we may just lose that status."

Chapter Twenty Two

When Nicholas and Geoffrey returned from delivering toys and gifts to the children on the island, Claire and Heather were waiting for them with a tasty platter of appetizers, and Irish coffee.

"Thank God you didn't bake us cookies!" said Geoffrey. "Every kid on this island left us cookies."

"Well you didn't have to eat them all," said Heather.

"Excuse me; I didn't want to hurt the little urchin's feelins."

"Well from the bulges in Nicholas's pockets, I don't believe he ate very many of his."

"Never mind, you guys," said Claire. "It's almost midnight, and soon it will officially be Christmas day; the very first Christmas for the four of us together."

"Shall I open a bottle of Champagne, my love?" asked Nicholas.

"Most certainly darling, this Occasion definitely calls for champagne; somehow, Irish coffee just doesn't seem appropriate."

Back at the main house, Leo and Ciara were on their

balcony making their own toast. Leo said that he could not be happier than he was at this very moment.

Ciara said that being reunited with Leo and Claire, as a family, after so many years, was a dream come true.

"To a most joyous occasion," said Leo.

"And many more to follow," said Ciara.

As the clock struck midnight, the sky seemed to light up, as if every planet in the universe had set off its own fireworks. It was a sight that would not soon be forgotten by the residents of the Island of Bliss.

Though all the children on the island were sound asleep, Leo knew that every adult on the island was lifting his or her glass in celebration of the love that everyone on the island shared for one another this first Christmas Eve.

"*To a Wonderful New World,*" said Leo. As he and Ciara lifted their glasses to the sky.

At the exact same time, Nicholas, Claire, Geoffrey, and Heather held their glasses, high in the air, and in unison said, "*To a Wonderful New World.*"

"Where did that come from?" asked Geoffrey.

"I believe we all know the answer to that," said Nicholas. "Who else, but Leo."

Soon, everyone on the island had retired for the night; they all knew that it wouldn't be long before the children would be awake, and ready to celebrate Christmas.

Chapter Twenty Three

Christmas Day was everything that Leo hoped it would be for everyone on the island. There was so much love and devotion among all the families, he had almost forgotten how little time there was left for this island family to be together. His little group of pilgrims would be leaving first thing in the morning.

"Attention everyone," said Leo. "Before we all sit down to this wonderful Christmas dinner, I would like to have everyone hold hands and remember why we are all here on this island as one very large family. We are here to love and be loved my children. Love really is all we need, and thankfully we have an abundance of it to give."

Everything was set up, buffet style, so after everyone had gotten a plate of food, and was seated, Geoffrey said that he couldn't allow anyone to start eating until he personally thanked all the ladies that had a hand in preparing this feast that seemed fit for a king, and he assured all of them that just in case there were any leftovers, he would be happy to help with putting them away.

"Away in his stomach," said Michael, and everyone broke into laughter, and began to dine.

After dinner, the Gray family took the children down to the stables for their final Christmas gift, and Nicholas and Geoffrey told Joseph and Amelia that they expected to do some horseback riding with the two of them when they returned to the island.

"We wish you didn't have to go," said Amelia. "But I promise that we will have special horses picked out for the both of you when you return."

"I'll even train them myself," said Joseph.

"Then I can't think of a better reason to hurry back home," said Geoffrey.

"Well, we could probably think of a least two more reasons," said Nicholas, as he and Geoffrey hugged the children and told them to hurry and catch up to the others.

"I'm really going to miss those little ones," said Geoffrey, as he and Nicholas watched the two of them run to catch the others.

"So will I, Geoffrey. I suppose that we really bonded with those two, from the start."

Just then, Claire and Heather walked into the room

and said that Leo was waiting for the four of them in the sitting room. When they arrived, Leo was sitting in a chair, that to Geoffrey, resembled a throne, *and rightly so*, he thought. To the right of Leo, was Ciara, in a chair that also seemed to be a throne, although a bit smaller, and more feminine.

"What a perfect day this has been," said Leo, as the foursome entered the sitting room; the first of many happy celebrations to come for all of us on the island."

Nicholas thought that Leo sounded a little less than sure of this, but maybe it was his own apprehension that was causing these feelings. After all, Leo was the reason that everyone on the island was here to begin with, and Leo certainly had powers that the rest of them didn't possess

"We are all immortal, Nicholas," said Leo, as if he heard Nicholas's thoughts. "It's our bodies that are not. William Blake summed it up quite well in this poem."

"Man was made for joy and woe – And when this we rightly know – Through the world we safely go - Joy and Woe are woven fine – A clothing for the soul divine"

"If we never had lows, then we would never have highs, I believe he considered joy and woe to be the human bodies that housed our souls, and when we shed these human bodies of joy and woe, the souls lived on."

"So that would mean that we are souls with a body, not bodies with a soul, right Leo?" asked Nicholas.

"Precisely, my boy, now if the four of you will please have a seat, Ciara and I would like to spend some time with you."

Chapter Twenty Four

The next morning, everyone that was scheduled to leave the island, gathered in the dinning room of the main house for a last meal together, so to speak.

Everyone sat in silence for what seemed like hours; that is until Nicholas finally spoke.

"This is not a funeral, this is just another rescue. Yes, there are more of us going on this rescue, but that's a good thing. Geoffrey and I will finally have some help."

"I know that this is your feeble attempt to make everyone feel better," said Deirdre. "And its working, isn't it everyone?"

It did seem to break the gloom that seemed to be hanging over the room, and it also caused a chain reaction.

"So now who is the chosen one?" asked Nicholas.

Everyone seemed to get a kick out of that one as Nicholas continued speaking.

"Seems that we were all chosen doesn't it?"

After breakfast, everyone gathered at the airfield to bid farewell to Nicholas and the others

"Now I think I know what the astronauts felt like when they left for each trip to space," said Geoffrey. "Proud, yet, also a little afraid."

"I think we will need that fear to keep us alert on this mission, Geoffrey," said Nicholas as they boarded the aircraft.

As the plane took off, Doc Holiday said that he could swear he could hear the song, "*Somewhere Over The Rainbow,*" in the background.

"I think we all hear it," said Claire. "And I think we all know who arranged for us to hear it."

Nicholas smiled to himself as he listened to the words, and knew that it could be no one else but Leo that would have arranged for them to hear this particular song as they headed into the most dangerous rescue mission they had been on thus far.

Claire said that she remembered hearing her father hum this song when she was small, and for some reason, it always made her feel safe.

"This must be my father's way of telling us all to be safe, and come home to him,"

"Leo has put a lot of faith in us," said Nicholas. "And I know that there is not one of us that will let him down so let us all relax and listen to this wonderful message from Leo."

Chapter Twenty Five

As the plane was landing in New York, Geoffrey made the comment that he could hardly believe that so much progress had been made in the world since his era.

"Air travel, space travel, sky scrapers, cures for diseases, and yet the fighting continues," he said. "Unbelievable."

Everyone agreed with Geoffrey, and Nicholas said that, if it were not for the unending wars, they would not have to be on a rescue mission today. He said that the world and its people would have continued to evolve until only love existed, and there would be no need for death.

"I know this will happen in spite of the fighting, but many have lost their lives over the centuries for no reason, and many more souls will lose their human lives before this is over."

A stretch Limousine was waiting at the private airport where they landed, and when they arrived at the hotel they were staying, Geoffrey asked if they could maybe see the Statue of Liberty, and the Empire State Building.

"Let's just get checked in and then see what is on the

agenda," said Nicholas. "We have a lot of work to do, in a much shorter period of time than we anticipated, so I don't think we will have much time for sightseeing."

Noticing that Geoffrey looked a little disappointed, he said that he didn't see why they couldn't at least see a few places of interest. This seemed to make Geoffrey very happy, *and after all*, thought Nicholas. This is the least he could do for this wonderful friend.

After Doc. Holiday took care of getting everyone checked in, he suggested that they all meet in about half an hour.

"That sounds perfect," said Nicholas. "Where do you want to meet?"

"I suggest we meet in the *King Cole Bar*. Supposedly, when the *Bloody Mary* cocktail landed here in America, it was perfected right here in the King Cole. Of course they call it the *Red Snapper* here, but it doesn't matter what they call it, to me it is the most perfect Bloody Mary I have ever tasted."

"Ya won't get an argument from me," said Geoffrey. "I have developed a taste for those things."

"Geoffrey," said Michael, "you know that you like all things edible or drinkable. I have never known you to have to develop a taste for anything."

Everyone laughed, and it was decided that they would all meet in the King Cole Bar, in half an hour.

Nicholas reminded everyone that even though their enemies were supposedly expecting them to arrive in Washington DC., they still needed to keep their eyes and ears open, and be alert at all times for anyone that seemed at all suspicious. Doc. Holiday booked the rooms, all in a phony name, and on the same floor, and said that we were here for a family reunion, so as long as they were out in public, they should act as if they are having a good time.

"That part comes pretty easy to this group," said Charles.

"That it does," said Michael, as they all got off the elevator, and proceeded to their designated rooms.

Nicholas, Claire, Geoffrey and Heather had adjoining rooms, so, it was only a matter of minutes before Geoffrey was knocking on the door that adjoined the rooms.

"It's unlocked," said Nicholas. "Come on in."

As Geoffrey came through the door, he asked Nicholas if he wanted to order anything from room service. He said that he saw it listed on the phone, and Heather explained what it was. "I really could use a little snack, Nickie, what about you?"

"I'll make a deal with you, Geoffrey, instead of calling room service, why don't the four of us go down to the bar, ahead of the others, and order some appetizers.

Besides, by the time room service got here, it would be time to leave anyway."

"Say no more Nicholas, I'll go get Heather and be right back."

"It really does take so little to please him doesn't it?" said Claire.

Chapter Twenty Six

By the time, the foursome had gotten down to the bar and ordered a drink and some appetizers, the others began showing up.

"We decided to go ahead and order some appetizers for everyone, since it would be quite a while before dinner, and it is really too late for lunch," said Nicholas.

"Geoffrey wanted to call room service didn't he?" whispered Michael.

"I heard that, Mikie," said Geoffrey. "And, as a matter of fact, not only did I want to order room service, I did order room service. I ordered one of every appetizer on the menu, and had them sent to your room, along with a very expensive bottle of champagne."

Everyone laughed, but you could tell by the look on Doctor Holiday's face, that he wasn't quite sure if Geoffrey was kidding or not.

"I presume that was a joke, Geoffrey," he said. "You all do know that I am responsible for the bill here."

"Ya know, Doc," said Geoffrey. "I use to take everything Chuck and Mikie said to me very seriously, until Nicholas filled me in on what dufusses these two were. I am now one of these dufusses. I learned at the foot of the masters."

"No problem, Geoffrey, you just answered my question, but now I'm thinking that I should keep an eye on the dufusses you learned so much from, especially the one that happens to be my son."

"C'mon, Dad," said Michael. "You know what a saint I am."

But before the Doc could reply to what his son said, there was a tremendously loud sound near by, that sounded very much like some sort of explosion, and the customers in the bar began to panic and run for the door.

Nicholas and his team remained at their table for a few seconds, and suddenly another explosion followed.

"Whatever you do, don't panic," said Nicholas. "This may have nothing to do with us, but if it does, then the first thing they will be looking for, is for us to exit the hotel by the front door. I want you all to get up slowly, and follow me into the kitchen."

As everyone followed Nicholas into the kitchen, people were scattering all over the lobby of the hotel. Nicholas and the others went out the back door of the kitchen, without much attention, because of all the chaos. After they made it outside, Nicholas told them to wait there while he and Geoffrey went around the corner to see what was going on.

As Nicholas and Geoffrey rounded the corner, they noticed a rather large crowed gathered in the street, and they could hear the sirens of the fire trucks headed in their direction.

"What's going on?" Nicholas asked a bystander.

"There was a gas explosion, and no one seems to know what caused it. It happened in the hotel across the street, but it was so close, that we all thought it happened in the hotel we are staying in."

"Are you staying at the St. Regis?" asked Nicholas.

"Yes, are you?" asked the stranger.

"Oh, no, we were just joining some friends for dinner, when we heard the first explosion. Have a good evening, and thank you for the info."

Nicholas and Geoffrey returned to the alley, behind the restaurant, only to find that the rest of their team had vanished.

"This can't be happening," said Nicholas. "I told them to stay put."

"You don't think they were taken, do you, Nick, we weren't gone that long?"

"I don't think they would have gone back inside without us, Geoffrey. I don't feel good about this at all."

Chapter Twenty Seven

Nicholas knew that if his team had been kidnapped, there had to be an element of surprise, because there were too many of them to just scoop up all at one time, so when he and Geoffrey went back into the hotel, he went directly to the front desk, to see, if by some slight chance, they had all gone back to their rooms, and left a message for him and Geoffrey.

There was still a lot of confusion inside the hotel, but the desk clerk said that someone did leave a message for him.

After Nicholas read the message, he asked the Clerk if he recognized the person that left the message.

"No, Sir, I didn't take any messages for you, but I'll find out who did take it, and let you know."

"Thank you, Mark, we'll be in the bar for a while if you find out."

"How did you know his name, Nick?"

"He had a name tag on his vest, Geoffrey, but that's not something that you were used to on the island, was it?"

After the two sat down at the bar, Geoffrey asked what the note said, and Nicholas told him that he wanted him to remain calm, so as not to attract any attention.

"Just tell me what the note says, Nicholas,"

"Promise me, first, that you will remain calm, because Claire and Heather's life may depend on it."

Geoffrey promised that he would remain calm; however, Nicholas could see something in Geoffrey's eyes that he had never seen before. He saw fear, and he knew that it was because he thought he might never see Heather again. He knew this because he was feeling the same for Claire.

As Nicholas began to read the note, he knew that his worst fear had come true.

> ***Nicholas, Please, do not underestimate us,*** *we know what you are here for, and we will simply not allow it. We have put many years into planning this takeover, and now that we have Leo's daughter, your wife, and Geoffrey's wife, nothing can stop us. The rest of your team should be walking into the hotel right about now. We have no need for them, but they will be proof, to you, that we do have Claire and Heather. Rest assured that no harm will come to them, as long as you do exactly as we say,*

***and for now, you are to go to your rooms, and
wait for the next message.***

Just as the note said, the rest of the team had returned.
Nicholas saw them in the Lobby, and he and Geoffrey
ran out to meet them.

Aside from looking a little spacey, they appeared to
be okay. Nicholas told them to follow him and Geoffrey
to the elevators, and remain very quiet.

The group did as Nicholas said and as soon as they
were in Nicholas's suite, the first thing he asked them was
if Claire and Heather were okay.

Doctor Holiday told Nicholas that as far as he knew,
they were fine. He said that while they were waiting, in
the alley, for him and Geoffrey, a huge black van pulled
up beside them, and sprayed them with some type of gas.
He said that was the last thing he remembered, until they
arrived back at the hotel.

"They let us all go, except for Claire and Heather, I'm
sorry, Nicholas, for both you and Geoffrey."

Hannah said she vaguely remembered Claire
whispering something to her as they took her and
Heather away.

"I'm pretty sure she said to tell Nicholas to go ahead
with the plan."

Nicholas questioned the others, but they all had the

same story. No one seemed to remember anything, except being sprayed, and riding in the van, back to the hotel.

Nicholas had no idea what to do next, except wait. He didn't see how he could continue on without Claire.

Chapter Twenty Eight

Suddenly the phone in Nicholas's suite started to ring, and he prayed that this was about Claire and Heather, but by the look on his face, Geoffrey knew that the news was not good.

"What is it, Nickie, are heather and Claire okay?"

"That was the desk clerk, and he has a package for me. He just wanted to make sure I was in my room."

About that time, there was a knock on the door, and when Nicholas answered the, a bellman was standing in front of him with a manila envelope in his hands.

Doctor Holiday tipped the bellman as Nicholas took the envelope and opened it, with a look on his face that Geoffrey had never seen before. He knew he must have the same look on his face, because he was terrified that he might never see Heather again, and he was sure that Nicholas must feel the same way about Claire.

"What is it, man, are our ladies okay?"

"They seem to be," said Nicholas, as he handed Geoffrey some pictures of Claire and Heather. "They want to know Leo's location, and they want us to take them to him. "This can't be happening, what are we going to do now?"

As if on cue, there was another knock on the door, and the bellman said that when he returned back to the front desk, there was another message, so he came right back with it.

After the bellman left, Nicholas opened the envelope and this time there was a look of relief on his face.

"It's from Leo. He says that he has gotten word of what has happened to Claire and Heather, and that we must comply with the wishes of the ones that have them. He also includes instructions for you, Doc. He says that you and the rest of the team are to round up the people that will be returning with us, and take them to the dock where there will be a ship waiting for us by the name of *One Song*. He says that Geoffrey and I are to tell the kidnappers to meet us at the ship, and that we will take them with us, on one condition. The ship will not leave until everyone that is meant to be aboard is aboard, that means Claire and Heather must be with them, or the deal is off."

"We cannot let these terrorists come with us Nicholas."

"You are right Geoffrey, we cannot allow them to board the ship with us; Leo is counting on us to find a way to sail without them."

Nicholas was supposed to leave the kidnappers a message at the front desk, and then proceed to the ship, so Doctor Holiday said that he would round the others up and leave right away.

"I'll see you on board, Nick," said Doctor Holiday. "Good luck to you and Geoffrey."

"Thanks, Doc, we won't be far behind you."

Nicholas and Geoffrey gave the Doctor a thirty-minute head start in order to make sure the rest of the team was safe and sound aboard the "*One Song*"

"I guess it's time we put our plan into action, my friend," said Nicholas, as he and Geoffrey approached the front desk of the hotel.

"What plan is that Nicholas?"

"I have no idea; I was just hoping that you might remember some of the ways you use to rescue Damsels in distress."

"Believe me, the villains in my day were not nearly as clever as the ones we are about to encounter, and to be honest, I always attacked first and asked questions later."

"I can't say that I have a plan that is any better than that Geoffrey."

"Nick, we have to come up with something, our ladies' are depending on us, and I cannot, no, I will not allow anyone to take them away from us."

"Geoffrey, these lunatics know we will do anything

to protect Claire and Heather, and they also know Leo would give them anything they desired before he would allow them to hurt his daughter.

For some reason Leo cannot leave the island; I don't know what that reason is yet, but I do know if we fail to save Claire and Heather, Leo will be forced to intervene, and I have a very bad feeling if that happens, we will never see Leo again."

Chapter Twenty Nine

After Nicholas and Geoffrey checked out of the hotel, they walked in silence toward the dock. Nicholas left a written message at the front desk for the kidnappers to meet him at the entrance to the dock in two hours. He thought this might buy him some time to come up with a plan to keep the kidnappers from boarding the ship, and at the same time rescuing Claire and Heather.

Geoffrey finally broke the silence.

"Nick, How long do we have?"

"Oh, about an hour and forty five minutes, and if you are wondering if I have a plan yet, well surprisingly, my friend, I do."

Nicholas started telling Geoffrey about an old movie he had seen, but before he could finish, Geoffrey began to yell.

"Please don't tell me that you are using some old movie plot idea to rescue Claire and Heather"

"Can you come up with something more original? Cause I sure can't.

It's not like I've ever had to do this before, Geoff, and I am as afraid as you are."

"I'm sorry, Nick, it's just that I cannot believe that any of this is happening."

"I can't either, Geoffrey, but we have to stick together, no matter what, and you need to trust me. All we have is each other at this point, and I can't think of anyone else that I would want to be beside me."

"I feel the same way Nicholas, in fact…"

"I'm sorry for interrupting, Geoffrey, but something is very off here. Look up at the sky and tell me what you see."

"Good Heavens, all hell is about to break loose!" yelled Geoffrey.

"Exactly," said Nicholas, "and I think this just might be the beginning of the end!"

By this time, the two had reached the "*One Song*," and as they boarded, Doctor Holiday was waiting for them with an extremely worried look on his face.

"Look Doc, Geoffrey and I don't have long, but I want you to listen to me very closely. If we are not back, in an hour, tell the captain to set sail. Something is terribly wrong here, and I can't risk everyone's lives, for ours."

"What about Claire and Heather?" asked the Doctor.

"They will be with Geoffrey and me, no matter what happens, I just don't want to jeopardize everyone's life if things get out of hand; besides, I have a feeling that Leo will make sure that we are safe, no matter what it costs him, so please promise me that you will wait no longer than one hour, from now, and then set sail, with, or without us.

"I promise, Nick, but I pray to God that it won't come to that."

On the way back to the entrance of the docks, Geoffrey asked Nicholas if he truly believed that Leo would save them should they not be able to make it back to the ship.

"I have no idea what Leo is capable of, Geoffrey, but I had to make sure everything went as planned in case something we are unable to return to the *One Song*. Everyone on that ship is vital to the new beginning on this planet, and I have to trust that we will live to be a part of it ourselves."

Shortly after Nicholas and Geoffrey reached the entrance to the docks, they noticed a helicopter approaching. Within minutes, it landed, and a man stepped out and began walking toward Nicholas and Geoffrey. As the man got closer, Nicholas thought he recognized him for some reason.

"Yes, Nicholas, I can tell by the look on your face

that you think I look familiar." said the stranger "guess you have a pretty good memory; because I too was transported to this century for a very different reason than you were."

"Who are you?" asked Nicholas.

"A clue, my son, I was present at your christening, and other important family occasions when you were very young."

"I remember now, you are my Uncle Jack, my father's best friend, and my Godfather. You were at my tenth birthday party and not long after, my father said you disappeared, and I never saw you again."

"That's right, Nickie, in the beginning, I was supposed to be a part of the same cause that you are involved in, but after reviewing all my options, I found that the grass really was greener on the other side, so to speak. Now, instead of standing beside Leo, I will be the one in charge, I will be the one that everyone is in awe of and I will be the Lord of Planet Earth."

Nicholas did not want to antagonize this man because he didn't want to risk Claire and Heather's life.

"Since the destruction of Planet Earth seems to be nearing, there is not much sense in haggling over much of anything Jack; in fact, whatever you want is yours, just return Claire and Heather to us right now, and I will make sure Leo doesn't interfere with your plans to become ruler of this planet."

"That's acceptable Nicholas; however, you know that I must accompany you back to the Island until the earth has been cleansed, I will surely perish if I stay here."

"You also know that when I return from the island, I will be bringing not only all the inhabitants of the island, but also the ones that are on the ship, and that includes you Nicky."

"You know something Jack, I really don't think the details of your takeover of Planet Earth matters right now, we will have plenty of time to discuss them once we sail."

Nicholas had no idea how this man knew all that he did about their mission, but at this point, he didn't care, he was ready to agree to anything to get Claire and Heather back safely, and worry about the rest later.

"No problem, Nick, I have my team stationed a few blocks away, and as soon as I give them the word, they will arrive here within minutes."

"Fantastic; then give them the word, but also tell them that the first two faces I want to see are Claire and Heather's. Until they are safe with Geoffrey and me, no one boards the ship, understood?"

"Of course Nicholas, consider it done."

Chapter Thirty

As Claire stepped off the helicopter, Nicholas managed to keep his emotions under control. The fact that Claire was safe was reason enough to take on the world, and that is precisely what he was about to do.

Geoffrey could hardly believe his eyes as he watched Heather walk toward him. *I couldn't believe I was lucky enough to have this wonderful lady marry me in the first place*, he thought. *I was so afraid that she was lost to me, forever, yet here she is, and there is nothing or no one that will ever take her away from me again.*

Nicholas and Geoffrey looked at each other as if they knew what the other was thinking, and as if on cue, a bolt of lightening appeared across the sky.

Claire and Heather were close enough by now to feel the electricity that seemed to surround Nicholas and Geoffrey, and as they held each other's hand, a calm spread throughout their bodies. They knew without even seeing each other's face that something amazing was about to take place, and as they reached the arms of Nicholas and

Geoffrey, simultaneously, they both felt something that neither had experienced before.

"Nicholas, I love you so very much, and I feel as if I could soar right into the heavens with you, at this very moment," said Claire.

"Geoffrey, you know how much I love you, and I believe that the heavens have opened up so that we may ascend," said Heather.

As much as Nicholas didn't want to loosen his arms from around Claire, he knew that he had to take control of the situation, and Geoffrey felt as well.

"My Angel," said Nicholas, "I do believe you can read my mind and I know without a doubt that you trust me, and that you love me as I love you, without condition, having said that, I ask that you please take my hand, and ask no questions."

"My lovely Heather, my lady," said Geoffrey, "I would never be able to hide my thoughts from you, nor would I ever want to, so knowing me as you do, you surely know that you can trust me with your life, so please take my hand my love, and never be afraid."

There was only silence for what seemed like an eternity, yet was merely only a few seconds. Claire and Heather were very much aware of what Nicholas and Geoffrey were trying to communicate to them. Claire also felt that she was beginning to come into her powers, because she felt such a surge of energy when she stepped out of the helicopter and saw Nicholas again.

Heather, on the other hand, couldn't figure out why she felt so strange. She knew she would evolve someday, but she never expected it to be so soon.

"That's enough," said Jack. "Let's get a move on; we need to set sail immediately."

"I agree," said Nicholas. "Time is definitely not on our side."

As everyone began to board the ship, Jack told Nicholas he wanted to meet with his team in the captain's quarters in one hour.

"You know, of course, the captain of this ship will now answer to me, and that my people will oversee every move you and your team make?"

"Look, Jack, your people greatly outnumber my own, so I don't believe there is any reason to hover over my team. I alone have the coordinates to reach the island, so it seems it would behoove you to treat my people, as well as myself, with the utmost respect."

"Agreed, Nicholas, just make sure everyone knows we will be watching every move you and your team make."

"No problem Jack; however, from the looks of the skies, I believe our biggest concern will be making sure that we all arrive on the island, alive."

Chapter Thirty One

Doctor Holiday and the rest of the team were waiting on deck as Nicholas, Claire. Geoffrey and Heather boarded the ship.

Nicholas could see the look of relief on the doctor's face, even though the doc was trying his best to keep his cool.

"Doctor Holiday, I'm sure you know Jack, and I'm also certain the least contact you have with him, the better, so if you will please have someone escort Jack and his people to their quarters, we will be able to set sail as soon as possible."

"Yes, Nicholas, I do know Jack, he was a man I use to call my friend, but I have more urgent matters that concern me right now. We need to board, immediately, and worry about everyone's quarters later, that is, if we even manage to make it out to sea."

As everyone hurried aboard, Doctor Holiday brought Nicholas up to speed.

"Nicholas, I know you have noticed how threatening the skies look, but I'm sure you haven't had time to really notice the unusual colors immerging from the clouds, and the changes in temperatures and wind direction."

"No sir, I'm afraid Geoffrey and I were pretty caught up in the rescue of Claire and Heather."

"I understand that, Nicholas, but I seemed to have ample time on my hands, so when I noticed all the strange weather changes, I met with the captain and he said he couldn't explain what was happening, and that everything he was seeing on his radar screen seemed virtually impossible. He said there were too many things happening all at once, and that we needed to set sail as soon as possible, or not at all. I decided then, to return to the dock once more to see if there was any sign of you and Geoffrey, and thank God you were there."

"Yes, Doc, thank God indeed, but I think the rest might be up to us."

Jack told Nicholas he would be accompanying him and Geoffrey on a visit to the Captain, and that Doctor Holiday, Claire, and Heather would remain with his team.

"I don't think so Jack, Claire and Heather stay with us from now on."

"Very well, Nicholas, but I'm sure you won't mind if the Doc takes my people to their quarters; oh and please don't forget Doctor Holiday, your daughter, Hannah, is also on this ship."

As Doctor Holiday lunged toward Jack yelling that he would personally be the one to execute him if anything happened to his daughter, Nicholas and Geoffrey each grabbed one of his arms and reminded him that Hannah's life was not the only one at stake at this time.

"Please calm down, Doc," whispered Nicholas. "The best thing you can do for Hannah is to be strong."

Nicholas noticed a calm come over Doctor Holiday, and as he and Geoffrey let go of his arms, he also caught a glimpse of fear cross Jack's face. Maybe there was more to the relationship between these two then Nicholas realized; well, whatever the story was, it would have to wait. Right now, Nicholas needed to make sure that the "*One Song*" left the harbor immediately.

As Nicholas and the others made their way to meet with the captain, no one spoke a word. It was if the Kaleidoscope of colors in the skies kept everyone mesmerized.

Claire was thinking about how many Fourth of July fireworks shows she had witnessed, and all she could compare this to, was the finale of every fireworks display she had seen, and then some. She wondered if Heather was thinking the same thoughts.

"Claire," said Heather, "It seems as if everyone in the world decided to celebrate the fourth of July at one time."

"I was thinking the same thing Heather, but they are either too early, or too late."

Nicholas was the first to notice that the ship had actually left the dock, and nudging Geoffrey, he whispered "I don't think there is much need in rushing to meet the captain, my friend. The "*One Song*" has sailed."

Chapter Thirty Two

Captain Bradford and his first mate seemed to be having a very serious discussion when Nicholas and the others reached the bridge.

"Excuse me, Sir," said Nicholas. "I'm sorry to interrupt, but I really must have a word with you. My name is---"

"I know who you are, Nicholas, Leo will be very happy to hear you are all safe. I was beginning to think you wouldn't make it in time."

By the way, I'm Captain Robert Bradford, and this is my first mate, William Cobb."

"Just call me Will," said Mr. Cobb.

"Very good to meet both of you."

Jack immediately stepped in front of Nicholas and introduced himself.

"Captain, my name is Jack Baker, and it is in your best interest that you pay close attention to what I am about to say. My team and I are taking over your ship, Captain, and I expect full cooperation from you and Mr. Cobb here, as well as the rest of your crew."

"Nicholas, what the blazes is he talking about?"

"I'm sorry, Captain, but we have no choice except to do whatever Mr. Baker says. His crew is holding the rest of my team hostage and I cannot risk any harm coming to any of them."

Nicholas went on to explain to the Captain that all Mr. Baker wanted was safe passage to the island.

"Leo will never allow him to step one foot on his island, Nicholas."

"I'm afraid Leo will have no more choice about that then you do, my friend," said Jack. "The Island of Bliss belongs to me now."

"Let's get one thing straight, Jack," said Nicholas, "If any harm comes to any one of us, you, my friend, will never reach the island."

At that, Jack threw back his head and let out a bellowing laugh.

"Nickie, my boy, are you threatening old Uncle Jack?"

"Well if he's not, I am," said Geoffrey, "and by the way, I don't believe he thinks of you as an uncle anymore."

"Boys, boys, boys, I'm really not a violent man, though I can't say the same for the rest of my team, however, as long as everyone does as they are told, there is no reason why anyone should get hurt."

"Tell me something, Jack," said Nicholas, "just what do you intend to do with us once we reach the island?"

"Well I don't intend to kill you, if that's what you want to know. As far as my long term plans, well, I'm not quite ready to reveal those to you."

Nicholas knew not to push Jack too hard at this time, and besides, he had another idea about how he might be able to win his trust.

"I would like to meet with you for cocktails before dinner this evening Nick," said Jack, "that is, if your beautiful bride doesn't mind. I promise I won't keep him very long, in fact, I would love it if you, Geoffrey and Heather joined us afterwards for dinner, at the captain's table of course."

"Sorry to disappoint you, Mr. Baker," said the Captain, "this is not your normal cruise ship; therefore, there is no *Captain's* table."

"Well I am terribly sorry to disappoint *you* Captain Bradford, but tonight there *will* be a captain's table, and *you* will not be sitting at it!"

"From now on, I suggest you be a little more respectful to the new Captain of the *One Song*. Have I made myself clear, Mr. Bradford?"

Nicholas knew the Captain was about to let his ego take over his common sense, so he jumped in between the two, and glaring right into the captain's eyes, he said.

"I'm sure you meant no disrespect to Mr. Baker, did you Captain? After all, there are many lives that depend on weather or not we can keep our tempers, as well as our egos under control."

The Captain, seeing the look on Nicholas's face, slowly gained his composure, and apologized to Jack, saying he meant no disrespect.

"After all, you are in command of this ship, sir, so if you would like me to arrange to have a special table set up for you and your guests, I will do so."

"I would like that very much Mr. Bradford. Oh, and be sure and tell your cook that should he get any wild ideas about poisoning any of the food while we are aboard, he might just think again. Who knows when I might decide to exchange dishes with another guest, or ask Nicholas to taste my food first."

"I will certainly remember that, Sir,"

Chapter Thirty Three

As Nicholas and Claire were being escorted to their quarters, Nicholas wondered how Jack knew about the "*One Song*." Leo said that the enemy would be expecting them to arrive *and* depart by air.

"Hey, Nick," said Geoffrey, peeking through the door that connected their quarters, "I know that we had to leave our luggage at the hotel so that if anyone were following us, they wouldn't suspect that we were leaving, but I had no idea there would be duplicate luggage waiting for us aboard the ship. I guess Leo thought of everything."

"Let's hope so, Geoffrey, but Leo had nothing to do with the luggage. I asked the Manager to have the luggage sent over to the ship. I gave him a rather large tip to make sure that no one knew who the luggage belonged to."

"I never heard you tell the manager anything,"

"That's because you were too busy rubbernecking."

"What do you mean, rubbernecking, Nicholas, what does that mean?"

"Something you do quite a bit of," said Heather, as

she grabbed Geoffrey's arm. "Let's get unpacked, and I'll explain what rubbernecking is to you."

As soon as Nicholas and Claire were alone, Nicholas said as much as he hated to admit it, he was truly mystified.

"I have no idea how Jack found out about the ship, and though I have a short term plan, I have no idea what to do if that doesn't work."

"Nick, there is no way that Jack can outsmart you, my Father chose you for a reason, and so did I."

Claire's words really did bring a smile to Nicholas's face, and as he readied himself to meet Jack for cocktails before dinner, he knew that he would have to give the performance of his life, and as he left the cabin, he turned to Claire and said.

"I know that you trust me, no matter what, and that is all that I can ask. I will see you soon, my love."

Claire was a little disturbed by the look in Nicholas's eyes because she knew though it was completely against his nature to hurt anyone, it would also be impossible for him to allow anyone to hurt the people he cared for, no matter what he had to do to stop them.

"Thank you for joining me, Nicholas," said Jack, I took the privilege of ordering you a drink. I'm sure you must be wondering why I asked to meet with you alone this evening so I will get right to the point."

"The truth is, Nicholas, I don't have many friends, in fact, I will go so far as to say that I have no friends at all. The only reason my team is loyal to me is that I pay them quite well."

"Surely you don't expect *me* to be your friend, Jack. You kidnapped my wife, not to mention people that I call *true* friends."

"Nicholas, I don't blame you for being upset with me, but I needed to get your attention, and show you that I was serious about what I plan to do."

"Well you got my attention, Jack, so tell me, what are your plans?"

"Not so fast, Nickie, we need to talk first. Contrary to what you must think of me, I'm really not a bad man. Your father and I were very close at one time; close enough, in fact, that he trusted me with your life."

"I guess my father was wrong about you, Jack, because what you are doing is not only wrong, but very dangerous."

"Nickie, there was a time when I would have done anything for your father, and still would if the circumstances were different, but no matter what I did, I could never quite measure up to him. He was Leo's right hand man, so to speak, and I always felt like an outcast when the two of them were together."

"I can't imagine Leo or my father ever making anyone feel like an outcast, Jack."

"You're right, Nicholas, they never ever treated me badly. I just envied the two of them so much. They seemed to have everything that I didn't. They had a family, they were admired and loved, and they were leaders. I wanted to be a leader, but your father always thought of me as a trusted friend, someone that he could count on, not someone that he looked up to and really respected like he did Leo, so I decided that I would find a way to make both of them look at me in a different way."

"The opportunity presented itself pretty quickly, because one evening I dropped by to see your father, and as I passed by the living room window, I saw he and Leo involved in what seemed like a very serious conversation. So I quietly let myself in, and stood in the foyer long enough to hear that Leo and your father had some sort of plan to take over earth sometime in the

future. I heard someone coming so I stepped back outside, and rang the bell as if I had just arrived."

"Well, needless to say, there was no more conversation about world takeovers after I walked into the room, and I knew then that I must find out what they were up to, and when the time came, I would be the one to take over the world, not those two. I would show them that I was just as smart as they were, if fact even smarter."

"Jack, they were not planning to *take* over the world; they were planning to *save* it. I'm sure Leo swore my father to secrecy."

"You know what, Nicholas, it really doesn't matter that much anymore because I have gotten a taste of power and I love it. I don't care about the world or the people in it, all I want is to rule, and trust me, I will be the leader, not Leo or your father, and if you are as smart as I think you are, you will join me; be my second in command."

Chapter Thirty Four

After Nicholas had gone to meet Jack, Claire hurried and dressed so she could have some time with Geoffrey and Heather before dinner. She knew how protective Geoffrey was of Nicholas, and somehow she was going to have to make him understand that he was going to have to remain calm tonight, no matter what.

"Knock, knock," said Claire, as she gently tapped on the door that connected their suites.

"Come in, sweetie," said Heather, as she opened the door. "Are you okay?"

"I'm fine, honey, but I do want to talk with you and Geoffrey before we go to dinner."

"Hey, I was about to knock on *your* door and see if you wanted to join us for a glass of wine before dinner, but from the look on your face, maybe I should be offering you something a little stronger."

"I guess I need to calm down a little bit before we

go to dinner, so a glass of wine would be great, besides, I need to have a word with the both of you before we go."

Claire proceeded to tell them that Nicholas said he had a plan that may only be a

short-term thing, but he didn't have time to explain. She said that the three of them would have to go along with whatever Nicholas said or did.

"Geoffrey, I know how much you care for Nicholas, so you must trust that whatever he does tonight is for the good of all mankind. Nicholas would never hurt or betray any of us. This will probably be the ultimate challenge for you Geoffrey. Doctor Holiday is already so upset with Jack, that Nicholas asked him and the others to dine in their cabins tonight. Please promise me that you will do whatever it takes to keep from losing your temper tonight."

Geoffrey made the promise to Claire, but said that if Jack caused any harm to anyone, he would have to do whatever it took to protect them.

Claire knew she couldn't ask for any more than that from Geoffrey, after all, he was brought here to protect Nicholas, even if it meant loss of his own life. She also knew he would put his life on the line for her and Heather.

"Thanks, Geoffrey, that's about all I can ask of you,

now I think it's about time we join Nicholas and Jack *McNasty* for dinner."

"I do have a more appropriate name for him, but I cannot say it in the presence of ladies."

Heather burst out laughing and said that she and Claire could probably think of a few words for Jack that Geoffrey had never heard before.

Claire started laughing also, but told Heather that it would be better if they kept them to themselves.

"I agree, ladies, and by the way, Heather, you can share those words with me later. After all, I am supposed to be learning as much about this century as I can."

Claire and Heather both giggled and said something about Leo having them banned from the island if he found out they were teaching Geoffrey things that were just not on his curriculum.

Nicholas noticed Geoffrey and the ladies headed toward his table, and he told Jack they could finish their discussion later, and he would appreciate it if he didn't mention anything they had discussed to Geoffrey and the ladies.

"I will need to explain everything to them in my own way," said Nicholas. "After all, Leo is Claire's father, and I want her to understand that what you are doing can benefit all of us."

"Good evening, ladies, Geoffrey," said Jack, as he and Nicholas stood to greet their guests. "I do hope you have brought a healthy appetite with you. I am told the chef has created some very special dishes for us."

Chapter Thirty Five

"I'm sure you have all been wondering why Jack wanted to meet with me first," said Nicholas, after everyone was seated. "Well it seems I may have been completely wrong about him Jack."

Geoffrey knew he was supposed to remain calm because Nicholas had some sort of plan, but he was afraid that if remained too calm, Jack would think it was a setup.

"Have you lost your mind, Nickie? This is the horrid creature that kidnapped our wives, and threatened to kill them!"

"I know," said Nicholas, "but it was just a ploy to get us to allow him to come with us. He had no intention of hurting anyone."

"Then why didn't he just ask you if he could come with us?" asked Geoffrey.

"Because there were others that were watching him, in fact they are on this very ship, pretending to be a part of Jack's team, when in fact, they are the very ones that really had Claire and Heather kidnapped."

"Jack has to pretend he is the leader, but he has promised that as soon as we reach the island, he will turn these people over to Leo, to be punished."

"Listen to me guys, I believe Jack. He was like a brother to my father, and he is my Godfather, after all. Please trust me, even if you don't trust Jack, yet."

"Nicholas, I don't know what this man said to you that caused you to trust him," said Claire. "And it does go against my better judgment, but if you really believe he is telling the truth, then I will stand by you in this."

"I do hope you know what you are doing, Nicholas," said Geoffrey.

"Does this mean you and Heather are with us?" asked Nicholas.

"This means we are with *you*, Nicholas, and I do hope you are not letting your heart rule over your common sense."

"Come on, Geoffrey, old boy," said Jack. "I would never do anything to harm my Godson, or his friends. Lets just have a nice dinner together, and Nicholas will explain it all to you later."

Geoffrey noticed that Nicholas winked at Jack, and that made him very uneasy, yet he knew Nicholas would never turn on him or his family. This had to be part of Nicholas's plan.

"I took the privilege of ordering a bottle of

champagne, Nicholas," said Jack. "I hope I wasn't being too presumptuous?"

"Not at all, Jack, after all, happy occasions call for champagne, and I do believe being reunited with my Godfather is a happy occasion."

Claire and Heather tried very hard not to look at each other because they both knew they would probably burst out laughing at Nicholas and Geoffrey. They knew Nicholas would like nothing better than to crack the bottle of champagne over Jack's head, and Geoffrey,

well, let's just say he would not only like to break the bottle over Jack's head, but he would also like to throw him overboard afterward.

Geoffrey was thinking about how much Nicholas was depending on him to keep a cool head, and he also knew as long as they all played along with Jack, they would be in much less danger than they would be if they defied him.

After Jack made a toast to rebuilding planet earth as a totally loving and peaceful planet, Geoffrey made the comment that he was starving.

Nicholas made a mental note *to thank Geoffrey later for being as normal as possible, under the circumstances.*

Chapter Thirty Six

After dinner, as everyone was about to leave the table, Jack said he had a small favor to ask of his new team.

"It is vital," he said, "to keep this new partnership among the five of us. Not even Doctor Holiday can be included. I cannot risk any of my so-called team finding out that I am

double crossing them, and sadly I don't believe the good doctor would be as understanding as you are. You see Nick, I believe deep down he was very jealous of my relationship with your father, if fact I believe he is the real reason I was kept out of the loop."

"Whatever you say, Jack," said Nicholas. "My priority is making sure we all make it to the island alive, and from then on it is Leo's call."

"Thank you, Nicholas, and may I say I had a most enjoyable evening with you all, so until tomorrow, I hope you all have a pleasant night. Oh, and by the way, the four of you are free to take a walk on the deck tonight if you like. I will tell my team that you have come over to our way of thinking. Just understand though, the rest of your team must still be under guard, and will not enjoy the same privileges as you do."

"I do understand," said Nicholas, "and don't worry; I will make sure Doctor Holiday behaves himself."

The walk back to the cabin was a very somber one because Nicholas was not really happy with what he was about to do and the others knew this.

"Why don't we meet back in our room," said Nicholas. "I think that I should speak with Doctor Holiday alone. I hate these lies, but I think it would be a little easier without an audience."

"Nicholas, thank God you are safe," said Doctor Holiday. I was beginning to worry."

"Please don't worry about me, Doc., I can handle Jack. I just wanted to make sure that you and the rest of the team were okay. Did you have dinner? Do you need anything?"

"Cut the crap, Nicholas, I need to know what happened tonight, and please don't whitewash it for me, Charles and Michael are beginning to get a little antsy also."

"Fine, Doc., Jack asked me to join his team, and I refused. The only reason he is allowing me any freedom is because he knows I won't do anything to put the rest of you in harm's way, and I believe he thinks I might change my mind. He knows you would never join up with him, but he can't be sure about me."

"Nick, I'm sorry I snapped at you but…"

"Forget it, Doc., we are all on edge. None of this is going according to plan, and I am afraid Leo can't help us out of this one. I get the feeling he can't leave the island."

"Nicholas, Leo is far more powerful than any of us knows, and whether or not he can leave the island, I believe his powers can."

"I certainly hope so, because I could sure use his help about now. By the way, where are your body guards, Doc?"

"They are in the suite next door, trust me, they are never very far away, but it's not like they have to hold a gun on us at all times, they have made it known that if one of us tries anything, they will simply kill one of our team, and unlike them, they know we care about each other."

Nicholas really felt terrible about not being able to tell the Doc what was really going on, but too many lives depended on his discretion. He knew the Doc would go along with Nicholas's plan, but he just couldn't take any chances."

As Nicholas was about to leave Doctor Holiday's cabin, he caught a glimpse of a strange blue light outside the balcony doors. As he turned around and headed toward the balcony, all hell seemed to break loose.

I'm the only one that has free reign at this point, thought Nicholas.

Chapter Thirty Seven

"What the hell is going on?" asked Jack to Captain Bradford. "I hope you didn't pull some stupid stunt like changing the ship's course."

"And why would I do that, Sir? After all, I am on your team, or have you forgotten?"

By this time, Nicholas had made his way to the helm of the ship to speak with the captain, about what was going on, but seeing Jack in what seemed to be a rather heated discussion with Captain Cobb, he decided to hang back and see if he could hear some of the conversation.

"How could I possibly forget?" said Jack. "I'm paying you enough. I just wish I had not had to kidnap Nicholas's wife, but I didn't have a choice. If my team and I had just shown up on this ship, Nicholas would have guessed that you were part of the conspiracy."

"I guess we really don't have to worry about that anymore, do we Jack; after all, Nicholas is on your team now, isn't he?"

"I'm not sure I am ready to disclose everything to

Nicholas at this time, Captain until I o make sure that he really is on my team."

"You haven't even included me in the entire plan, Sir."

"Soon, Captain Bradford, very soon, but we have more pressing matters to attend to now."

Nicholas knew this was the perfect time to make his entrance, so he burst into the room as if he just arrived.

"Captain Bradford, what is going on?" asked Nicholas.

"Precisely what I would like to know," said Jack.

Nicholas pretended to be startled when he heard Jack's voice.

"I arrived only moments before you, Nicholas," said Jack, "and the Captain assures me he is right on course, however, I have my doubts."

"For God's sake, Jack, why would Captain Bradford change courses? He does work for Leo, remember?"

"Yes, Nicholas, I do remember, and that is precisely why I thought he might have changed courses. Maybe Leo had an alternate plan in case the original plan went wrong. What if the captain is headed for another island?"

"You have lost your mind, Jack, Leo's daughter is aboard this ship, do you honestly think he would risk having her brought to another island, besides, there are no other islands even remotely close to Bliss."

"Bliss, ah yes," said Jack. "Of course Leo would name his island Bliss, why not?"

"What are you talking about, Jack, the island is pure bliss, why wouldn't Leo name it that?"

But before Jack could reply, a lightening bolt struck so closely to the ship, that Nicholas felt as if every fiber of his being was energized, and he knew that if everyone on the ship did not band together; no one would live long enough to reach the island.

Chapter Thirty Eight

"What the devil was that?" asked Geoffrey, as he hurried toward the balcony of the suite. "It looked like a flashing blue light."

"This is definitely not the "*Love Boat*," Geoffrey," said Heather, as she, Geoffrey, and Claire walked out onto the balcony. "I just hope we all live long enough to take one of those cruises."

"I just hope Nicholas is safe," said Claire. "We still have a few more days until we make it back to the island, and I am not sure how long any of us can keep up this charade. It really is much harder to pretend than to tell the truth."

"Wow, is it just me, or does it feel as if the temperature just dropped about twenty degrees?" asked Heather.

"I'm not sure I can control this ship much longer," said Captain Bradford. "It's as if it has a mind of its own."

"Just let the ship go where it wants to go," said Nicholas. "I have faith that Leo is in control at this point, and we all want to reach the Island of Bliss."

Jack started to laugh and said that Nicholas was right. He said that Leo had probably programmed the ship to head directly to the Island of Bliss.

"This is not necessarily a bad thing for you, Jack, after all, you do want to take over the island, and if you don't have to depend on Captain Bradford to get you there – whoa, am I seeing things or are the windows beginning to frost up?"

"The temperature is dropping outside," said Claire, "But Father did warn us that there would be many changes in weather patterns before the end,"

"Yes, but we were supposed to be back on the island before all these changes started taking place." said Heather.

"I need to go check on Nicholas," said Geoffrey, "he should have been back by now, but I don't want to leave you two alone."

"Then we'll go with you," said Claire. "Jack did say we could leave our suites."

As Nicholas opened the door to the suite, he overheard the last part of Geoffrey, Claire, and Heather's conversation.

"Hey guys, I'm fine, but I could use a glass of brandy to warm me up."

As the three turned to look at Nicholas, they all

noticed a look on his face that none of them had ever seen before.

As Geoffrey poured Nicholas a brandy, Claire took his hand and brought him over to sit beside her, and after he took a sip of his brandy, Claire asked him if Doctor Holiday had given him problems.

"You look as if there is something you dread telling us," she said.

Nicholas told them that it wasn't the Doctor that was giving him problems, it was Jack. He told them how he had overheard Jack and the Captain in a conversation, and learned that Captain Bradford is part of Jack's team, not Leo's.

"Jack doesn't know that I am aware of this," said Nicholas. "But now it's hard to know who to trust"

"Maybe he's pretending to be on Jack's side, like we are Nicholas," said Geoffrey.

"I'm afraid not, my friend, he is strictly in it for power and monetary gain, just like Jack. What I don't understand, though, is how Leo could have chosen someone so weak and uncaring. Something just doesn't fit, and I'm going to find out what it is before we reach Bliss."

Chapter Thirty Nine

Early the next morning, Nicholas quietly slipped out of his and Claire's suite, after writing a note telling Claire that he was meeting Jack for coffee, and would join her for breakfast.

"Not so fast, Nicholas, you cannot slip away from me that easily. I had a feeling you were going to try and sneak out this morning, so I slept with one eye open, so to speak."

Nicholas stopped in his tracks, and turned to see Geoffrey standing before him, in cut off jean shorts, two different colored socks, sandals, and a long sleeved shirt.

"I'm not sure whether to laugh, or to send you back inside to change clothes," said Nicholas.

Heather opened the door to the hallway before Nicholas could say anything else, and handed Geoffrey a pair of long jeans, tennis shoes, white socks, and a sweatshirt, and as Nicholas tried to stifle his laugh, Claire opened the door to their suite, and when she saw Geoffrey changing clothes in the hallway, she really lost it.

"I'm sorry, Geoffrey," she said. "It's just that the last

thing I expected to see this morning was a man changing clothes in the hallway."

"Tell the truth," said Heather, "It was the one red and one green sock that did it to you, wasn't it?"

"I don't think this is so funny, I tried to dress in the dark so that I wouldn't wake Heather."

"I need to hurry and meet Jack before breakfast, Geoffrey, so if you're coming with me, I suggest you shake a leg, and by the way, my darling, Claire, I left you a note. I love you and will see you at breakfast."

"You know, Geoffrey, old boy," said Nicholas as he and Geoffrey headed off to meet Jack. "You need to know that socks are never worn with sandals, even if it's Christmas, and they ARE red and green. Do you have any idea how much Charles and Michael would have tortured you if they had seen you this morning?"

"Good morning, gentlemen," said Jack, as Nicholas and Geoffrey entered the dinning room. "I trust you slept well."

"As well as could be expected under these frightful circumstances," said Geoffrey.

"And what frightful circumstances are you speaking of Geoffrey?"

"Geoffrey is just a little concerned about the storm that seems to be approaching, right Geoffrey?"

"Nicholas is right, Jack, I've never been fond of storms."

"Don't worry, Geoff," said Jack, "we have everything under control. Now if you two will please have a seat at my table, I will go see what is keeping Captain Bradford."

As soon as Jack was out of hearing range, Nicholas told Geoffrey that he needed to be very careful about what he said in front of Jack.

"Jack may not trust us entirely, and I don't want to give him cause to worry that we are not both totally in agreement with him. Just follow my lead, okay?"

By this time, Jack had entered the dinning room and was headed back to the table. He said Captain Bradford would not be joining them.

"It seems you were right to be concerned about the weather, Geoffrey. The captain says it looks as if we are in for some pretty ominous weather. He suggests we have everyone join us in the dinning room as soon as possible, so Geoffrey, if you would, please go and make sure that everyone joins us within the hour. Nicholas will stay with me."

After Geoffrey left, Jack told Nicholas that things were escalating much faster than anticipated. He said he didn't want to alarm Geoffrey because he didn't want him to cause the others to panic.

"Nicholas, I saw the radar screen when I was with the captain, and I can honestly say that I am extremely concerned. I knew that the weather conditions would eventually start to deteriorate, but I never believed it would happen this quickly, and with such force.

"Does the captain have any idea where we are?"

"Unfortunately he was never able to change the course of the ship, after losing control of it last night. He said it was like a huge magnetic field was drawing it in the direction it wanted it to go, and short of causing the ship to capsize, there is nothing he can do."

"Then I suggest we all pull together as a team, Jack. I will inform my group about the impending danger, and I assure you they will cooperate. Our first goal is to survive, and then we can worry about the rest later.

Chapter Forty

"Nicholas, what is happening?" asked Claire, as she entered the dinning room with the others

"I have very little time to say what I need to say," said Nicholas, "So everyone please listen closely."

"Jack is meeting with his team, and has allowed me a short time to meet with mine. Earth's conditions are deteriorating at a rate so much faster than we anticipated that we may not reach the island in time to be saved, but this is only speculation."

"I have great faith in everyone in this room, and I know you trust me as well, so I am asking that you all focus on one goal, and one goal alone. That goal is to save humanity, and in order to do this, we must all realize, that though Jack and his followers are strictly looking for power and monetary gain, they are still human beings. I know you all have great love and forgiveness inside of you, but you are going to have to reach much deeper than you ever have before in order to make this mission as successful as Leo knew it would be. The future of earth's children is in your hands."

"Nicholas, the captain says according to the squall line on the radar screen, we need to prepare for high seas and strong winds as soon as noon today," said Jack, as he entered the dinning room. "I trust that you have informed your people as to the urgency of this matter."

"My people, no, my friends are aware of the impending danger, and I am happy to say that they are not only prepared to do whatever is needed in order to protect everyone on this ship, they are also honored to be a part of the rebirth of planet earth.'

Nicholas could tell that he struck a cord with Jack, because for the first time since he had been reunited with him, he could actually see a glimpse of his Uncle Jack.

"What can you do to prepare for something like this? asked Jack.

"I believe we can answer that question," said Michael. "You see, Chuckie and I are quite the sailors, and though we have never navigated a ship of this magnitude, we believe that we can be of more help to Captain Bradford than anyone else on board."

"Permission to go to the helm, Sir?"

"What do you think, Nicholas, do you need them here, or do you think they would be of more help to the Captain?"

"Jack, I honestly believe that Captain Bradford could do much worse than these two, I have had the honor of sailing with both of them, and they are not only very knowledgeable, but courageous as well."

"Very well, Nicholas, I do trust your judgment of people, so I say they may join Captain Bradford."

As everyone gulped down as much coffee as possible, Nicholas made sure that Claire was no farther than three feet away from him

"I will not go through the angst of wondering if you are okay, or not, again, my darling Claire, there is nothing or no one more important to me than you."

Claire was about to tell Nicholas that she was not about to let him out of her sight either, when suddenly the ship began to lurch and everyone started grabbing hold of anything they could to keep from being thrown to the other side of the ship.

"Better call Captain Bradford and find out what's going on," said Nicholas.

"That won't be necessary," said Captain Bradford, "I was on my way down here to tell you that I no longer had any control whatsoever of the *One Song* and that we should prepare to abandon the ship, when I encountered Charles and Michael. They said that you sent them to see if they could help, but when I told them what I saw on my radar screen, they agreed that we needed to alert you as soon as possible."

"Well, what did you see?" asked Nicholas, but before

Captain Bradford could answer, they heard someone say "Oh my God, what the devil is that thing?"

Nicholas turned to see Jack motioning for him to come see for himself, and as he got closer to the exit door where Jack was standing, he could see the horror on his face.

"Everyone listen very carefully" said Nicholas "I have no idea what that is out there, and we cannot waste time trying to find out so head for the life boats, NOW!"

Chapter Forty One

"It's freezing out here" said Heather, as she and Claire followed closely behind Nicholas and Geoffrey. "It's a good thing the lifeboats are enclosed."

"Just make sure that we are all in the same lifeboat," said Claire.

Jack was just a few steps in front of Nicholas and when they reached the lifeboats he asked Nicholas if he would allow him to come with him aboard his lifeboat.

"I know I don't have the right to ask, Nicholas, but I have some things to say to you and I may not get another opportunity."

Nicholas said that he had no problem with it as long as the others didn't object.

Everyone agreed that the most important thing right now was everyone's safety, and as the men began to lower the lifeboats and make sure that everyone was accounted for, Nicholas said that they should all turn on their flashlights, and to use their flares if they get into trouble.

"God bless you all," said Nicholas as he prepared to board his lifeboat "I will see you soon."

Once everyone was safely inside their lifeboats, Nicholas noticed that the *One Song* had totally disappeared. No one else seemed to notice, so he kept quiet about it until Geoffrey broke the silence and asked if anyone had noticed that the ship seemed to have disappeared into thin air. They all said they had, but thought it might just be the weather conditions making it appear to be gone.

"No it's gone," said Nicholas, "and it didn't sink, it just disappeared into thin air, and I believe that whatever that gigantic thing that looks like an ice burg had something to do with it."

Claire asked if he thought it was drawn into the ice burg and if so, why were they not being pulled toward it.

"I think it's because it believes we are still aboard the ship," said Nicholas.

"That's like saying it's alive," said Jack, but as soon as the words left his mouth, the waters became calm, the sun came out and right before them was the Island of Bliss.

"I guess Leo was taking care of us after all," said Nicholas.

"And I guess this is where I either stay in the lifeboat

and take my chances in the new world, or face the punishment I deserve," said Jack.

"Nicholas, I did an unforgivable thing when I kidnapped Claire and Heather. I would never have harmed them, but you didn't know that and neither did they. I wanted power so badly that I never stopped to think about the pain I was causing. I just believed that all of you wanted the same things that I did until you allowed me to come with you on your life boat. It was at that moment that I realized how wrong I was about Leo and your father all those years ago. They were not trying to shut me out they were just trying to protect their families. They couldn't share certain things with me because it might have put me at risk also. I see that now, but I was so blinded by my jealousy that I turned into a monster."

"Looking at all of you now, I know what I have to do. I deserve to be punished so I am turning myself in and please know that I ask for no mercy."

By this time, Doctor Holiday's boat had reached the island and he and his family were already on shore.

Nicholas noticed that Captain Bradford and the others were headed away from the island, and Jack made the comment that he sincerely hoped that they survived long enough to see the truth."

"Welcome home everyone" said Leo as he held out

his arms. "And a special welcome to you Jack since this is your first time to visit our island."

"I think you need to arrest me or something" whispered Jack "Obviously Leo doesn't know what I've done."

"Oh trust me, he knows," said Nicholas as he watched Claire run into Leo's arms. "You see, no one can set foot on the island of Bliss unless they are pure in spirit, and obviously you meant every word that you said on the life boat or you wouldn't be standing here with us."

"Are you saying Leo is some kind of psychic and he was aware of all that was happening with all of us?" asked Jack.

"Something like that, just trust me when I say you have been punished more by your own guilt than you will ever be punished by any of us, especially Leo.

"My God, how could I have been so blind all those years ago?" I believed your father was pushing me aside for Leo and the Doc, when all along, they were all protecting me. I must find a way to make it up to them."

Chapter Forty Two

On the walk back to the house, Claire told Leo she never wanted to leave Bliss again, and he reminded her she had many more missions ahead of her that would take her away from the island, but that Bliss would always be her home.

Nicholas asked Leo if he knew what the object was that pulled the *One-Song* inside of it and why the bad weather suddenly ceased after the ship disappeared.

"I felt as if it thought we were still aboard the ship and that it had captured us."

Leo said that the object was actually a force field that came about because of all the conflicting weather conditions, and it would have taken all of you as well, but the energy field surrounding Bliss was much stronger and the moment we entered that field, it ceased to have control over us."

"You see, Nicholas, Bliss is not really an island on earth, it actually exists in another dimension, and the more pure souls that arrive here, the more powerful Bliss becomes. I needed you all to come back to the island."

"I think I finally understand now why you cannot leave the island," said Nicholas.

"What do you mean, Nicholas?" asked Claire, but just as he was about to answer, he looked into Leo's eyes, and he knew that this was not his story to tell, and before Claire could repeat her question, she spotted Ciera walking toward her.

"Welcome home, my darling," said Ciera. "I am so happy to see all of you back safe and sound."

By this time, Ruby came bursting out the front door with her large arms open wide to hug any and everybody that she could wrap her arms around.

Next in line for their hugs were Molly, Maggie and Catherine.

"Hey, save some of those hugs for us," someone yelled, and as Claire and the others turned around, they saw the Gray family headed their way.

Joseph and Amelia were especially excited to see Nicholas, Claire, Geoffrey and Heather, their newly adopted aunts and uncles.

"By the way," said Geoffrey, "where is my mother?'

"Oh, Lady Margaret and Mr. Lovejoy were right behind me," said Amelia.

"I see them coming now," said Geoffrey, "looks like he has not left her side since we left."

"That is about the size of it," said Ruby, "and don't

you dare say a word to discourage her. They are a lovely couple, and you could do worse for a stepfather."

"And speaking of couples," said Nicholas, "where are my planet hopping parents?"

"On a mission, as usual," said Ruby. "Leo will fill you in later, I'm sure."

"Listen up," said Ciera, "everyone is invited to a welcome home party later this evening, but for now, I think this group needs a little rest." So as everyone made their way to their quarters, Catherine and Maggie said they would show Jack to his room and bring some food up to everyone within the hour.

"Okay, Claire," said Nicholas, "before you even bother to ask me about what I said to Leo about knowing why he cannot leave the island, please understand that I had no right to say that."

Claire said she was so tired that it really didn't matter anyway.

"I'm sure Father will tell us when he is ready."

Later, when the welcome home party was over, Leo requested a meeting after dinner with Nicholas and his team.

During dinner Geoffrey asked Nicholas what he thought Leo meant when he said he wanted to talk with them about what happened on the ship.

"I guess we are about to find out, Geoffrey, here he comes now."

"I trust dinner was enjoyable," said Leo

"As always," said Nicholas. "Molly made all our favorites."

Leo then said that dessert and coffee would be served on the beach deck, and he asked that everyone join him there as soon as they were done.

As soon as everyone had their coffee and dessert, Leo said he realized that everyone was still pretty wiped out from everything they had been through, but that there was not much time left to complete this mission.

"First of all, I want you all to know I am very proud of the way you handled everything that was thrown at you, and I do not want you to think for one moment you let me down."

"Nicholas, you actually cut off the snake's head when you allowed Jack to be with you in the life-boat. You see, the others' lost what they thought was their power when they had to abandon the ship, and their leader went with you, and rather than join forces with him, they chose to take their chances on their own."

"I know you feel you failed because you didn't bring survivors back, but you are wrong. There are survivors, and they will be arriving soon. The *One- Song* is now under your Father's command, Nicholas, and because of all of you, it is now safe for him and your mother to rescue the survivors and bring them to Bliss."

"Then you were controlling the ship the whole time?" asked Nicholas.

"No, not the whole time, only when it came near enough to the energy field of Bliss, and I was only able to control it because of all of your energy combined with mine. You see, the more souls we bring to Bliss that are pure in spirit, the larger the energy field grows."

"I guess I was right when I said I thought I knew why you couldn't leave the island" said Nicholas "You are the island's energy Leo and if you leave, the island ceases to exist. You created Bliss."

Chapter Forty Three

No one said a word for what seemed like an eternity, and as if it was meant to be, Jack stood up and with tears streaming down his face, he asked Leo to forgive him.

Leo said that there was no need because he was actually the one person that he sent his team to bring back.

"You see, I knew you would never hurt anyone, Jack, but I had to let the others believe that you would, and for that I am truly sorry."

"But why would you want me here after all I have done to try and destroy all you stood for?"

"Because you have always stood for the same things I have, you just got lost along the way. You are a very powerful man, Jack, and now it's time you used that power to help us rebuild planet earth."

"There is more I would like to share with you, Jack, but it can wait for another time."

"Now, everyone get some sleep tonight and Nicholas, I would like to meet with you, Jack and Geoffrey tomorrow morning."

Walking back to their quarters, Claire said that she wondered what else there was about her father that she didn't know.

"I know I shouldn't be surprised about anything that concerns my father, but tonight was next to unbelievable."

"You know, Claire, it finally makes sense to me. Leo said that Bliss is in another dimension and that the more souls we bring to the island, that are pure in spirit, the stronger the island becomes. I believe the island is the result of Leo's energy."

"Remember how there were storms on the island when you first arrived, but as more and more souls arrived, the storms became less and less? Well I believe that Leo's energy alone was enough to sustain Bliss, but as the population grew, the field of energy around the island grew; therefore pushing the storms farther and farther away from the island. In fact, I would not be surprised if the island is actually growing in size."

"Oh this is just too much for my brain to digest tonight, Nicholas. A good night's sleep in my own bed is all I want to think about until tomorrow."

The next morning Nicholas left Claire sleeping and just as he was about to descend the stairs, he heard footsteps behind him. Turning, he saw Geoffrey coming down the hall, with Jack following close behind him.

"Guess we all had the same thought," said Nicholas.

"If you mean getting up early enough to watch a magnificent sunrise from an island so filled with natural beauty that it takes your breath away," said Jack, "then I guess we did all have the same thought."

"I actually got up early because I thought I smelled Molly's pancakes and sausage cooking, but what you said sounds good too, Jack."

Nicholas and Jack doubled over in laughter, and Nicholas said that for the first time since they arrived back on the island, he truly felt like he was home.

As the three headed toward the kitchen for coffee, Nicholas began telling Jack about all the wild and wonderful times he and Geoffrey had shared together.

"I cannot tell you how much it has meant to me knowing that Geoffrey had my back during some pretty scary times, he is truly my brother."

As the three neared the kitchen, Geoffrey began smiling from ear to ear.

"I guess I wasn't dreaming when I said I smelled Molly's pancakes and sausage"

"No, Geoffrey," said Molly, "you were not dreaming. Leo asked that I prepare an early breakfast for the four of you, and I know how much you love my pancakes."

"And sausage," said Geoffrey.

"Yes, Geoffrey, and sausage, you didn't think I would forget the sausage did you?

Nicholas suggested they head out to the beach deck and wait for Leo, but when they arrived, they saw Leo headed back from the beach.

I wonder if he ever sleeps thought Nicholas.

By the time Leo reached the deck, Nicholas has poured him a cup of coffee.

"Thank you, my boy, now if you will all join me at the table, we can get this meeting done because by the smells coming from the kitchen, breakfast is almost ready and I would not want to be the cause of Molly's pancakes getting cold."

"I don't blame you, sir, but Molly wouldn't be the only one you would have to face."

"Ah yes," said Leo as he looked at Geoffrey's big smiling face.

"First of all I want you all to know that I met with my dear friend Doctor Holiday last night because I did not want him to think I was excluding him. He is going to be very busy training new comers to the island, at least the ones that are already involved in the medical field."

"You three, however; along with Michael and Charles, are going on a very special mission of your own."

"There is a group of beings that are being held captive; these beings are an integral part of my plan to rebuild the new world. Some will serve as teachers of the arts, some as historians and others as architects and builders."

"Charles and Michael are going along because they know the planet quite well and will serve as your guides and interpreters."

"This planet is about to destroy itself, much like the planet earth did so it is vital that you rescue these beings before that happens."

"Now it has recently come to my attention that if we intend to save these beings, we must move immediately, because the planet is deteriorating faster than anticipated. I'm sorry you won't have more time to spend with your loved ones, but the future of the new world depends on you, any questions?"

"Leo," asked Geoffrey, "did you say the words Planet and beings?"

"I did, Geoffrey, but please don't let that worry you, Charles and Michael will be right beside you every step of the way."

"That's what I was afraid of," said Geoffrey.

Nicholas, by the time you return from your mission, your father and mother will have brought back some very prominent doctors and scientists themselves. They of course will be an integral part of Doctor Holiday's team. He will share healing powers with them unlike any they have ever seen, and when the devastation is over and the new world begins, they in turn will go out into the new world and train others."

"Now if there are no more questions, we will get on with this meeting. Geoffrey and I have an appointment with a huge stack of pancakes."

Nicholas & Jack stood dumbfounded, while Leo and Geoffrey went off to breakfast.

"I don't know about you, Uncle Jack, but I'm not all that excited about this mission."

Jack put his arm around Nicholas's shoulder, looked at him and smiled.

"This will definitely be a dangerous mission, Nicky; however, knowing that we are going to be on the same side, somehow makes me feel so much better."

"You are a force to be reckoned with, my boy."

Chapter Forty Four

After breakfast Jack said he would like to meet with the Doc if it was okay with Leo he said he felt he owed him a personal apology.

"Before you go," said Nicholas, "can you tell me what the connection is between you and Doctor Holiday?"

"A woman, Nicholas, the doctor and I were in love with the same woman. She chose him of course, but when he found out that I was the one that had kidnapped Claire, it infuriated him but he takes his oath seriously. Even if you would have let him attack me, I don't believe he could have gone through with it."

Leo told Jack he could find Doctor Holiday in the medical facility.

"In fact, if you wouldn't mind, Geoffrey…"

"Say no more, Sir, let's go Jack."

After Geoffrey and Jack left, Nicholas asked Leo why he couldn't remember him when he was a young boy.

"If you were around at the same time as Jack then I should remember you also."

"Nicholas, your father made sure you were never around when we had our meetings."

"I see, but there is one more thing that I don't understand. You spoke of a man that was your friend and you said that he was part of the plan; that man was Jack, wasn't it?"

"Yes, the man I spoke of was Jack; however, he disappeared before I could fill him in on what part he would be playing in our plan to save the earth."

"He said he overheard you and my father planning to take over the world so that must have been the night he disappeared."

"Yes, the very night we were going to fill him in."

"Nicholas, your father was my right hand man, but Jack was the one I planned on taking with me to Bliss. He would have been next in command on the island, while your father and mother handled things from their end."

"Are you going to tell him, Leo?"

"Yes, as a matter of fact, I intend on telling him this afternoon, now go find your wife and spend the day with her, and that's an order."

"Yes Sir, you don't have to tell me twice." and as Nicholas left the beach deck, Leo smiled, and wondered if Nicholas and Claire would ever figure out that he had always planned for Nicholas to be the one to bring Claire back to the island; however having them fall in love with one another was an added bonus.

Later that afternoon, Leo asked Jack to join him for a walk on the beach and just as they reached the water's edge, Leo said there were some things he needed to tell him in private. He told him that he did share this information with Nicholas because he felt he deserved to know.

"Jack, before Bliss existed, I confided in Ayden about my plans for Bliss because I wanted him to know that I intended to ask you to come with me. I had other plans for him and Deirdre, and we met several times in private to discuss those plans."

"The night you overheard the two of us discussing what you thought were plans to take over planet earth, was the same night I intended on telling you about Bliss, but you disappeared."

"How did you know I overheard the two of you?"

"That's not important, Jack, the important thing was that you should have trusted Ayden and me, but you let jealously and then greed take you over. I could have stopped you and told you that you were making a huge mistake but I needed for you to realize this on your own and I believe that happened on the journey back to Bliss. You could have stayed with your team but you felt the need to be with Nicholas and you really had no idea why."

"Jack, you finally let go of that demon when you decided to come to Bliss and take whatever punishment I chose for you and when you made that decision, you secured your position on the island of Bliss."

"I have no words, Leo. There are no words."

"Of course there are words, my friend. The only words you have to say are yes, or no. Do you accept the position of standing by my side for eternity?"

"Yes, oh yes I do accept that position Leo and please know that I will never again let go of my faith in all that is divine."

"This is truly my awakening, Leo. I finally have a knowing of the spiritual connection we all share and I am finally at peace."

Chapter Forty Five

Early that evening, the ones that had made the journey together decided to have their own private celebration and as they all joined together on the Waterfall deck, Nicholas proposed a toast to the success of their journey.

"Some of you may feel that we didn't accomplish much on our journey, but we actually accomplished more than you realize. We fulfilled a wish of Leos', a wish for a prodigal son's return."

Leo then appeared with Ciara by his side.

"I too would like to make a toast," and as Catherine and Maggie began pouring glasses of champagne, everyone gathered around Leo.

"To the island of Bliss and all that it stands for!"

Every one of you are a part of Bliss, a part of me. I am filled with such love and appreciation for you because you are the pure in spirit, and I thank you for all that you have done and are about to do for soul kind. I say soul kind instead of man kind because we are eternal souls that live on even after our physical bodies expire. Know that I love you all."

As everyone lifted their glass to the toast that Leo made, Nicholas noticed that Jack stepped forward until he was standing by Leo's side, and after Leo touched his glass with Ciara's glass, he turned to his right and touched his glass with Jack's.

After taking a sip of champagne, Jack stepped forward and turned toward Leo and said. "I won't waste everyone's time with details of how I came to be allowed onto the island of Bliss because you all know that Leo does not judge, he allows."

"That said, I would like to thank Leo, and all of you for allowing me to be a part of Bliss."

"I will not waste your time with promises, I will only say that I have experienced an awakening and nothing could ever compare to the energy of love that I feel from all of you."

"Thank you, Leo, for believing in me, and thank you, Nicholas, my godson, for not condemning me, and thank you both for allowing me to be a part of this journey with you."

"I hope no one else has a toast," said Geoffrey, "I am much too emotional for all this." and as everyone took a sip of their champagne, Nicholas told Geoffrey that his comment was the perfect thing to say in order to loosen everyone up, and I suppose that was true because Michael put on some island music and everyone seemed to take a deep breath at the same time and then the party started.

"You see, Geoffrey, timing is everything, and your timing was perfect."

"Hey, you are scaring me, Nick. You said the words Geoffrey, timing, and perfect all in one breath."

"Loosen up, Geoffrey," said Heather, "I believe that the *Order of the Sleepless Knights* should now assume the dance position."

Nicholas then turned to see that Jack was standing all alone; Leo had disappeared, once again.

"So, Jack, where did Leo go?"

"Probably as far away from all the noise as he can get, but hey, I'll hang out awhile if it's okay with you." and with that said, everyone approached Jack and personally welcomed him to Bliss.

Chapter Forty Six

Early the next morning Nicholas awoke to an unfamiliar sound and as he jumped out of bed to see what was going on, Claire, startled by his sudden move, sat up and yelled at Nicholas.

"What on earth are you doing, Nick?"

"Didn't you hear that strange noise, Claire?"

"No, I didn't, but I hear it now and it sounds like a ship's horn."

"The *One Song,*" said Nicholas, "the *One Song* is back. I didn't realize they would be arriving so early."

Nicholas knew that it would take some time to dock the ship; he hurried and showered so he could be there to greet his parents.

"Take your time, Claire," he said, as he kissed her goodbye, "I'll go play catch up with mother and father and meet you for breakfast."

Claire just shook her head and laughed as she watched Nicholas almost hurt himself trying to get through the door.

No wonder he is Santa Claus, she thought, *he gets so excited over so many things that most people take for granted.*

As Nicholas reached the dock, he noticed that Leo and Doctor Holiday were greeting the new arrivals as they disembarked the ship. He noticed that his mother and father were nowhere in sight and just as he was about to ask Leo where they were, Leo turned to him and said

"Ayden and Deirdre are waiting for you aboard the ship, Nicholas."

I didn't even have to move my lips, thought Nicholas, *Leo knew exactly what I was going to say, so why am I surprised?*

As Nicholas boarded the *One Song,* he saw his mother and father waiting for him.

"You better not tell me that you are leaving again before we get to spend some time together," he said.

"Not a chance," said Ayden. "We will be here for awhile"

"I am so happy to see the two of you; we have so much catching up to do. Unfortunately I am the one that won't be here for very long."

"I'm sure we will have a day or two to visit before you leave for another mission," said Deirdre. "Let's make the best of it, my son. When all of our missions are over, we will have plenty of time to spend together."

By this time Claire appeared and said Molly was preparing a brunch.

"This will be a very private get together," said Claire. "Just Nicholas and I and my very adventurous mother and father –in-law. I suppose Nicholas told you we will be leaving soon for another mission?"

"Yes he did tell us," said Deirdre as she hugged Claire, "and we do appreciate your arranging for the four of us to have brunch together, but don't you want Leo and Ciara to join us?"

"Actually it was their idea that the four of us spend some time catching up on what has happened since we last saw you and besides, they are planning a special dinner for the six of us tonight."

"In that case," said Ayden, "lead the way because I am starving."

As the four headed toward the main house, Nicholas couldn't help thinking about his next mission and that caused him to feel a little guilty. After all, his parents had just returned and all he could think about was where he was going next, and who they would be bringing back.

"Well you are the son of Ayden and Deirdre after all," said Leo.

Startled, Nicholas turned to see Leo standing next to him.

"I won't even ask where you came from and how you knew what I was thinking."

Leo told Nicholas he need not feel guilty because his father and mother were having the same thoughts as he was.

"Leo is right," said Ayden. "Your mother and I are so happy to see you and spend time with you, but like you, we know there are many, many, souls out there that are depending on us to save them. There will be plenty of time for all of us to be together after all our missions are completed."

By this time they had reached the main house and Molly greeted them on the front porch and announced that brunch would be served on the waterfall deck.

"And it is a particularly spectacular brunch if I do say so myself. In fact, I had to make sure that Geoffrey had already eaten; otherwise it might not be there when you arrive. You know he has an uncanny sense of smell."

"Only when it comes to your cooking, Molly," said Nicholas

"You are so full of it, Nicholas, but just to be safe, I guess I should go find Geoffrey and maybe give him a little afternoon snack."

Chapter Forty Seven

After everyone had eaten, Deirdre said she and Ayden were going to take a much needed rest and would see Nicholas and Claire at dinner.

"Claire," said Nicholas, "I have a wonderful idea, you and I and the beach. We have not been alone in a very long time and I think we both need to get away from everyone for a few hours."

"That sounds heavenly, Nicholas", but she had no longer gotten the words out of her mouth, when Geoffrey appeared.

"Nicholas, Claire, I'm so sorry to interrupt, but I do need to have a few moments with Nicholas if I may. I promise I will not keep him for long."

Nicholas was about to protest but Claire intervened and said that it was quite alright because she needed to speak with her father before they left for the beach.

After Claire left, Nicholas told Geoffrey he had better make it quick because he and Claire had planned to spend the afternoon together at the beach.

"Alone at the beach," he said.

"Nicholas, you know I would not interrupt if it were not important and after you hear what I have to say, I believe you will agree that I was right to come to you with this."

"Charles and Michael just told me that they are going with us on our next mission."

"And that is a problem because?"

"It's a problem because Michael says that he believes we are going to another planet."

"Nicholas, I have never been on another planet. It has been hard enough for me to adjust to this century and now Leo wants me to adjust to another planet?"

"Not adjust, just rescue a few aliens and leave," said Michael, as he approached Nicholas and Geoffrey.

"How did you know where I was, Michael?"

"I figured that you would freak out and run to Nicholas when I told you that we may be visiting another planet so I thought I should come and explain a few things."

"Michael, there was no reason to share your thoughts with Geoffrey," said Nicholas. "That is unless you were trying to agitate him. You really have no idea where we are going on our next mission do you?"

"No I do not, Nicholas, but I'm sure that we will be visiting another planet sooner or later."

"Geoffrey, you really must take everything that Mikie

says with a grain of salt, you know that he lives to get a rise out of you."

"Well then, a rise he shall receive."

Geoffrey lunged toward Michael and began yelling.

"You best start running man because I am right behind you and I intend to make YOU rise."

Claire returned just in time to see Michael running toward the beach with Geoffrey not so far behind him.

"I do not even want to know what that was all about, let's just go to the beach, but in the opposite direction of where those two are headed."

"The island is quite beautiful, isn't it?"

Startled, Jack turned to see Ayden standing behind him on the waterfall balcony.

"Yes, Ayden, Bliss is quite breathtaking, but I cannot imagine why you are even talking to me. I'm sure you would rather throw me over this balcony."

"As a matter of fact I would rather throw you over the balcony than ever speak to you again; however, Ciara threatened to never speak to me again. You see, she is much more forgiving than I am, and she does her best to keep me grounded so if Nicholas and Ciara can forgive you, and Leo believes in you, than I should be willing to give you the benefit of the doubt as well."

"Yes, but it is different for you, isn't it, Ayden? You and I were like brothers, then, I went and did the unthinkable. I hurt your son, my Godson, and when I did that, I severed the bond between us. I cannot blame you if you never trust me again."

"Well, Jack, my brother, I'm afraid you will have to be a martyr somewhere else because I do trust you. Don't get me wrong, I hate that you made Nicholas think that Claire was in danger. Leo told me the whole story. He said you thought that he and I were conspiring to take over the world and that we left you out of the loop."

"Ayden, an apology would sound lame so I won't even bother to utter the words"

"On the contrary, Jack, an apology is just what I need. I need for you to tell me why you didn't come to me in the first place. How could you think that I would ever turn my back on you, the man that I loved as a brother, the man my son called Uncle Jack, the man that I trusted to raise my son should anything happen to Ciara and me?"

"Then an apology you shall get"

"I apologize that I didn't trust our friendship enough to come to you with my fears. I let jealousy take me over. I let my self imagine the worst. I felt sorry for myself, telling myself that given a choice of partners, who in their right mind would choose me over Leo, and from there it mushroomed. The anger and the fear took over, and from that came the greed and feelings of revenge.

I had convinced myself that you and Leo were the bad guys that wanted to take over the world for your own selfish reasons, and convincing myself of this allowed me to plan my own takeover, that is until I saw Nicholas."

"Ayden, I knew in my heart that I could never kill anyone, but I couldn't let anyone else know that so I created the cold hearted, mean spirited Jack that would take over the world and annihilate anyone that got in his way."

"I guess seeing Nicholas for the first time since he was a little boy, brought back all the memories of you and I and our bond, a bond that I broke and though I tried hard to ignore those feelings, they eventually won out. I was ready to take the punishment I deserved and yet what I received was forgiveness, from Leo, from Nicholas and Claire, Geoffrey and Heather and from Ciara."

"You know, Jack, Leo said he believes you are truly sorry for what you did and he is willing to trust you enough to be his first mate so to speak, so I have to believe that you are sincere, and while I do trust Leo's judgment, I wonder if you have really paid for what you did to me and my family."

"Of course I haven't paid, Ayden, it will be a very long time before I feel that I have paid for my transgressions;

however, I will continue to do whatever it takes to find the old Jack again, and bring him back home."

"I cannot ask for more than that," said Ayden, as he turned and walked away leaving Jack to reflect on his past.

Chapter Forty Eight

The next morning Nicholas noticed that everyone seemed to be hustling and bustling more than usual and when he asked Ruby what was going on, she just shook her head and smiled.

"You know, Nicholas; this is the day I have been waiting for since I arrived on Bliss. Doctor Holiday and Hannah are in the medical facility working with the doctors and nurses that will soon be teaching medical students of their own on planet earth."

"Your mother and father are here with you, Leo and Ciara finally have their daughter back, and there are children here that will grow up on the new planet earth with a very different view than their predecessors."

"Can you imagine what a difference these children will make in the lives of their children as they share what they have learned on Bliss? It just gives me chills, Nicholas."

Nicholas laughed out loud and said that he had never seen Ruby so emotional.

"I am not laughing at you, Ruby; it's just so heartwarming to see you this relaxed about the future."

I do agree with you that these children have so much to offer their off-spring. What terrific parents they will be; wonderful grandparents as well. It's like a new beginning with the Crème de la Crème of spiritual Gurus."

"Now I have to laugh," said Ruby, "Spiritual Gurus? That is so not your normal choice of words."

"And where in the world did you hear the saying, *so not?*"

"I know more than you think I do, Nicholas, by the way, what are you doing having breakfast alone?"

Nicholas explained that Claire was having breakfast with her mother and that he just wanted some alone time.

"I really want to take a walk on the beach and think about what a lucky man I am and also think about different ways to sabotage Alien Monsters.

"Excuse me, Nickie, did you say alien monsters?"

"Never mind, Ruby, it was just a joke."

As Nicholas headed toward the beach, he could hear Ruby muttering, *It damn sure better be a joke, Mr. Nickie, cause I'm an alien myself and I would take offense if I thought you were serious.*

Nicholas turned around to face Ruby and began walking backwards and throwing kisses.

"Ruby, my love, I could never think of you as anything but the most precious alien in the universe, you know that."

Ruby chuckled to her self and whispered; *yes I do know that, Nicholas, I do know that.*

The next morning came much too quickly for Nicholas and Claire.

"I can't believe you have to leave today, Nicholas," said Claire, as they were getting dressed for breakfast.

"Me either, Claire, but the sooner I go…"

"I know, the sooner you will return and you better return without an extra head or something."

"Claire, I'm surprised at you, you know there are no one bodied aliens with two heads, only two headed aliens with one body"

"I'm telling Ruby you said that, Nickolas"

"She won't believe you because in her eyes, I can do no wrong."

"We'll see about that," said Claire, as she headed towards the door.

Nicholas ran after Claire, yelling *come back here, woman,* but before he could stop her, she threw open the door and standing before the two of them was Leo himself.

"Father, we didn't expect to see you standing there."

"Who did you expect to see, daughter, one of Robin

Hood's Merry Men? The whole *come back here woman,* thing kind of threw me."

Nicholas and Claire looked at each other and then at Leo, but neither one of them uttered a word.

"Never mind, darling, I'm terribly sorry to interrupt but I do need to speak with Nicholas before breakfast."

"Of course, Dad, I know the drill, see you two at breakfast"

As soon as Claire was out of ear-shot, Leo told Nicholas that his mission was being aborted.

"It seems that the prisoners that were being held on planet Palatine have escaped, and are headed for a small planet near Palatine named, of all things, Refuge.

Nicholas, you and your team will have to intervene before the prisoners of Palatine land on Refuge, because it is a very small planet and the Palatineans are capable of blowing it up if they get near enough to do so; I'm afraid you will be leaving right away."

"So you're saying that we are going to have to rescue these people in space, before they land?"

"It won't be easy, Nicholas, but Charles and Michael can are both ace pilots when it comes to spacecraft."

"Which brings me to the fact that I have never even seen a spacecraft, much less been aboard one and let's not forget the fact that Geoffrey and I know nothing whatsoever about outer space."

"I realize that Charles and Michael are from another planet, but won't they have their hands full?"

"Yes, Nicholas, they will, and that's why Jack is going with you. He is an expert astronomer; he knows the planets and their location better than anyone I know. You and Geoffrey will be in very good hands."

"Leo, please don't get me wrong, I am not questioning your judgment, it's just that Geoffrey is even greener than I am when it comes to technology in today's world, not to mention the whole solar system and he is going to be turning to me for answers."

"I just want to make sure I have those answers."

"I understand, Nicholas, and if you like, I will speak with him before you leave."

"Not necessary, sir, you gave me enough information, just enough to be dangerous I might say, but Geoffrey will never know that."

Chapter Forty Nine

Nicholas found Claire on the beach deck having coffee with Geoffrey and Heather.

"I know that look," said Geoffrey. "It means I'm going to have to skip breakfast, right?

Nicholas was about to tell Geoffrey that Ruby would probably throw some of her homemade biscuits in a bag for him when suddenly, she appeared, bag in hand.

"Leo told me earlier that you would be leaving earlier than expected, Geoffrey, so I packed all your favorites."

"I can attest to that," said Lady Margaret, as she walked up the steps to the beach deck. "You certainly never had food that good when you were a little boy, and for that matter, neither did I."

"I wanted to come and see you off, my boy, and to tell you how proud of you I am."

"Thank you, Mother, and please don't worry about me, I'll be back in time for supper, I hope."

Everyone started laughing because Geoffrey always brought out the child in them and as Lady Margaret and

Heather were giving Geoffrey their goodbye hugs, Claire pulled Nicholas aside.

"Hey, space cadet; and I say that with love, hurry back to Bliss, I miss you already."

"Come here, Mrs. Space Cadet." And as Nicholas held Claire in his arms, he could see over her shoulder that Jack, Charles and Michael were headed across the lawn to what looked like a helicopter.

"Guess it's time for us to leave, Geoffrey." As the two headed for the helicopter pad, Heather and Claire ran after them.

"Don't worry," said Claire, "we are only going to follow you to the helipad, not much room for stowaways anyway."

Nicholas's mother and father were waiting for him as he approached.

"I was wondering if you were going to show up before I left."

"You know better than that, Nickie."

"Yes I do, Mother, as a matter of fact, I was sure the two of you would be waiting here to make sure my shoes were tied and I brushed my teeth."

Seriously you two, I am glad to see you; however, I will be back before you know it."

"We're counting on it, son."

"See ya soon, pop."

Nicholas hugged his father and mother, gave Claire one last kiss, and boarded the helicopter.

"Please come back to me, Nicholas," whispered Claire as she blew him a kiss.

Leo was waiting on the other side of the island, and as the helicopter landed, Nicholas could see him standing next to a disk shaped object and he knew that it must be the spacecraft that would take them on their next mission.

There wasn't a doubt in Nicholas's mind that Leo would be there to see them off because that's who Leo was.

I don't really know who or what Leo is, he thought, *but I do know what he is made of, it's called unconditional love and you can't help but feel it whenever you are near him.*

After last minute instructions from Leo, everyone began boarding the spacecraft and as soon as the last member of the team had boarded, Nicholas turned to Leo, hugged him and began to board the craft himself, and as the spacecraft headed upward into the atmosphere, Leo looked up and said, *"take care, my son."*

Chapter Fifty

"Unbelievable," said Nicholas, as the spacecraft soared through space. "Are you okay, Geoffrey?"

"Piece of cake, Nickie, this thing moves so fast that you can't even tell it's moving and speaking of a piece of cake."

"Geoffrey, I would hold off on that piece of cake if I were you," said Jack, "you might just want to get acclimated to space before you eat anything."

Michael asked that everyone please stay buckled in until they cleared the earth's atmosphere.

"You can have all you want to eat after that, Geoffrey; that is if you can hold onto it."

Geoffrey opened his mouth to ask Michael what he meant by that remark but Nicholas interrupted.

"Geoffrey, in his own lame way, Michael was trying to tell you that once we leave the earth's atmosphere, we will all be weightless, even the food that Ruby Packed."

"Thanks, Nickie, but why didn't the dufus just say that in the first place. I know all about gravity. Talk of gravity began in the fourth century with Aristotle, then in the beginning of the Seventeenth century, Galileo had a theory of his own; based on the ideas of the Polish astronomer Nicolous Capernicus, but it was Einstein's theory of gravitation that revolutionized twentieth century physics."

"Geoffrey, how did you…?"

"Know so much about gravity? First of all, I lived during the days of Galileo and the rest I learned from Leo, now is there anything else you boys need to know?"

Nicholas smiled and shook his head as the others stared at Geoffrey like he had two heads.

"What's wrong with you fellas? You look like the three stooges, now turn around and quit starin' at me or you won't be getting any of the grub that Ruby packed."

"How come you always lapse into your old speech patterns when you get riled up, Geoffrey?"

"I'll show ya riled up, Mikie, when we dock with the other spacecraft. Maybe I'll just kick ya butt out into oblivion, and no one will ever have to hear your whiney voice again."

By this time, everyone was laughing hysterically.

"See Geoffrey, if it were not for you and me, what would these guys do for entertainment?"

"Okay guys," said Jack, "I think it's time we actually talked about the reason we are on this mission together in the first place."

"I know that all of you are very trusted friends of Leo's, just as I was at one time. I would like to regain his trust, as well, and the only way I can do that is to do my best to make this mission a success without anyone getting hurt."

"I will risk my life before I allow anyone of you to lose yours and I think that Leo is counting on that."

"You're not saying that he sent you along to be a decoy if we needed one are you? Because Leo would never do that."

"No, Michael, that's not what I'm saying, I'm saying that Leo is counting on me to be as brave and selfless as you all are, and if I'm not, than who better to let him know this than his most trusted *Impossible Mission Team.*"

"Part of what you said is correct, Jack. Leo must trust you because he would never allow you to be part of our team if he didn't."

"You see, Leo would never risk our lives just so he could be sure you could be trusted, and besides, he wasn't kidding when he said you would not have been allowed to set foot on Bliss if you were not pure in spirit."

"Michael, are you saying that an island can tell if someone is pure in spirit or not?"

"No, I'm saying that Leo can tell, and I assure you that

he knew before you got within a mile of Bliss whether or not you were sincere."

"Guess I just can't shake the guilt of what I did to him and his family."

"Guilt is not allowed on Bliss, Jack, so I suggest that you start concentrating on right now and forget the past."

"I agree, Michael," said Geoffrey, "so I'm getting something to eat, RIGHT NOW."

Charles said that a bite to eat sounded good to him, as well.

"And with Geoffrey around, a bite is all…"

"That's enough, Charles, I think it's time to stop picking on Geoffrey and go over our rescue plan."

"Jack, I didn't know ya cared, but I do appreciate it."

"No problem, Geoffrey, the five of us are quite diverse as far as our personalities, but each one of us has a strength that when meshed together, could become a force to be reckoned with."

"Why else would Leo choose us for this mission?"

Chapter Fifty One

After everyone was done munching on the food that Ruby had packed for them, Nicholas made a statement that stunned the other four.

"Has anyone of you ever given thought to the fact that everything we are experiencing is just plain bullshit?"

"Nicholas? What the hell are you talking about?" asked Geoffrey

It's all bull, Geoffrey, life is but a dream."

"Nicholas, this is not like you at all, man."

"Well it's certainly not like *the me* that you know, but what if *the me* that you know just isn't real at all?"

"Now ya scarin' me, bro. I'm thinkin' that outer space just don't agree with ya."

"It has nothing to do with outer space or inner space, Geoffrey, it has to do with Bliss and Leo and the fact that we can travel through time. If your body was real, it couldn't do that so I'm thinking that your body is just an illusion, something that we only imagine is there. I believe that we use it to communicate with other bodies because we believe that we need our bodies but in reality, we don't need them at all."

"You've all seen Leo and some of the others appear and disappear at will and haven't you noticed that Bliss seems to be growing larger by the day?"

"Everything we are experiencing is beyond the physical."

"Yep, that's why it's called metaphysical, Nick."

All eyes turned toward Michael as he spoke.

"We are all evolving, spiritually, Nicholas, some faster than others. Leo just happens to be the most spiritually evolved of all of us at this time but we will all be there sooner or later."

Geoffrey sat with his mouth hanging open, staring at Michael.

"What the hell did you think was happening to us, Geoffrey, did you think Leo was magic or something? Magic just doesn't exist, but miracles do and whether you realize it or not, we are all performing miracles every single day."

"If that's true, Mikie, then I am going to perform a miracle, right now, and see to it that you are silent for the rest of the trip."

"Geoffrey, you cut me to the quick. How can you be so hurtful?"

"Stop it, Mikie, you are the smart ass, you know, you are always picking on me."

"That's because I like you so much, Geoffrey. Don't you know that people always pick the prettiest rose in the garden? Not that I'm saying you're pretty or anything, but in reality, you are the kindest of all of us because you are the most childlike and before you get upset about that, I'm simply saying that you are the most genuine being of any I have ever met, with the exception of Leo and Nicholas, of course."

"I don't quite understand all of what ya just said, Mikie, but I think there was a compliment in there somewhere."

Nicholas burst out in laughter and everyone else followed suite.

Jack said that Geoffrey should be very flattered by all that Michael had said.

"I just hope someday that someone says those things about me."

"Well you're never gonna smell like a rose, Jack, that's for sure," said Geoffrey and again the rest of the crew began laughing, but only for a few seconds because what happened next caused everyone aboard the spacecraft to practically cease breathing.

"What the devil was that?" asked Jack

"Looked pretty big to me, whatever it was," said Charles.

Michael said they should be in close proximity to the spacecraft they would be docking with, so hopefully whatever went passed them, would keep going.

"Doesn't look like that's going to be the case," said Jack. "It's coming back and it looks like it going to ram us."

"Not happening, Jack, not as long as I'm driving this ship." And as quickly as the words left his lips, Michael dropped the spacecraft so quickly that the rest of the crew said that they felt as if they had left their stomachs behind.

"Hold on guys, I got one more trick up my sleeve."

Geoffrey was wishing that Michael had asked him to hold on before he made that last move, but thankful at the same time that he had warned him about this one because it was a doozie.

The space craft seemed to suddenly shoot straight up, take a sharp left, a sharp right, dip down and after that, Geoffrey thought he was going to loose consciousness.

"Okay guys, we lost him."

"You almost lost us as well, Mikie."

"Geoffrey, is that any way to thank the being that just saved your non existing body?"

Geoffrey cracked a smile and mumbled a thank you to Michael.

"Don't think this is forgiveness for all the smart little remarks you have made to me in the past, Mikie."

"Don't worry, Geoffrey, I won't."

"And don't think that rose thing get's you off the hook either."

"Of course not, Geoff."

"Fine, I just wanted to make that clear."

"It's crystal clear, Geoffrey, now do you mind if we continue with our mission?"

Chapter Fifty Two

After about five minutes of silence, Nicholas asked Michael why anyone would try and run into them.

"Wouldn't that mean certain death for them as well?"

"Ever heard of suicide bombers, Nicholas? It seems that some concepts never change and no matter how hard we try to save the planets, there are always those that want to take them over at any cost. They have no regard for human life and no belief in afterlife so their sole purpose is to have all the money and all the power because that is the meaning of life to them."

"Hold up everyone, Leo is calling in," said Charles.

"Go ahead, boss."

"Charles, I have finally been able to contact our prisoners."

"They are waiting to dock with you."

"Jack will direct you to a safe haven where you will wait until it is safe to return to Bliss." "Take care, boys, and I will see you all very soon."

"Leo, wait," said Geoffrey, "Remember the Star Wars movies Nicholas and I watched?"

"I do remember, Geoffrey, what about them?"

"Well, I kind of feel like you should say something more profound than, *see you soon.*"

"Oh, I get it, Geoffrey, are you ready?"

"Ready, Leo."

"May the force be with you, Geoffrey."

"Thank you, Leo, see ya soon."

Surprisingly, no one laughed. I guess they all knew that Geoffrey, as brave as he was, just needed a little encouragement from Leo that everything would be okay, after all, he was from a time in history where death surrounded him on a daily basis. He was a knight in King Arthur's army.

Nicholas finally broke the silence.

"Geoffrey, you are my best friend and my brother, but if you don't get me back to Bliss in one piece, you will have to deal with Claire."

This time everyone did start laughing, even Geoffrey.

"All right, hotshots, it's show time," said Jack, "refuge is just around the bend so that means our refugees must be waiting for us on the other side."

As soon as Michael docked with the other space ship, Jack, Nicholas and Geoffrey prepared to board.

"Make it quick, boys," said Charles, "my radar says that company is headed our way. "You have about five minutes."

As the three boarded the other craft, they found four very frightened beings that seemed to be on the verge of exhaustion.

Seeing this, Geoffrey told Nicholas that if he and Jack could each help one, he could manage the other two, and in an instant, Geoffrey had one under each arm and began carrying them back to their own craft.

"Welcome aboard the…."

"*Sky King,* Geoffrey."

"Yes, I know you think you are the king of the sky, Michael, but what's the name of our ship?"

"*Sky King* is the name of the ship, Geoffrey. I'll explain that one when we get home, better yet, I will share my Sky King videos with you. We'll have a Sky King night, popcorn and all."

"Let's move it, Michael, our friends programmed their ship to continue on to refuge in order to throw their captors off."

"I'm already on it, Jack, just steer me in the right direction. By the way, what's the name of the planet?"

"It's called *Chameleon*, because it is the only planet in the universe that can actually disguise itself."

"Get outa here, Jack."

"I'm serious, Michael. This planet is virtually unknown to most people because it changes colors so frequently that it appears to be gasses in the galaxy."

"Cool, now all we need to do is find it."

"That is not a problem, Michael. You see that mass of different colors directly in front of you? That's Chameleon."

"Jack, are you sure? It looks like…"

"I know what it looks like, but trust me, it is our destination."

Michael headed straight into what looked like a massive rainbow and prepared to land, even though he saw nothing to land on.

Jack told him to drop the ship straight down and as he did, a huge mass of land appeared beneath *The Sky King.*

"Talk about *somewhere over the rainbow,*" said Charles, "even Oz didn't look this beautiful."

As soon as the words left his lips, he could see that Geoffrey was about to ask where Oz was.

"Oz is a fictitious place in a movie called *The Wizard Of Oz,* one of my very favorite movies; in fact I'll take you to see it when we get back to Bliss."

"Is popcorn included?"

"Popcorn, cokes and I'll even throw in a box of Mike and Ikes."

By this time the *Sky King* had landed and Geoffrey was so caught up in the beauty of *Chameleon* that he didn't ask what Mike and Ikes were.

Jack was the first to exit the ship so that he could see the faces of everyone else aboard as they experienced their first glimpse of this magnificent planet.

One by one they immerged and each one had a look of awe on his face; even the beings they rescued seemed to forget how very weak and weary they were as their eyes fell upon the magnificent beauty of this planet.

Chapter Fifty Three

"*Welcome to Chameleon, everyone.*" *said a voice that seemed to come out of nowhere.*

Geoffrey's eyes grew as big as saucers and Jack began to chuckle.

"Hello, again my, friend."

"Hello to you, Jack, and welcome back."

"I see you have some friends that don't appear to be doing very well, is that the reason for your visit?"

"That and the fact that we have some pretty nasty characters looking for us."

"I see, well let's take care of your friends first and we can discuss these unsavory characters later."

As everyone followed Jack, Charles and Michael said they couldn't believe there was a planet in the universe they didn't know about.

Jack said *Chameleon* was a planet that very few beings knew about, and for good reason, but before anyone could question him about his statement, a rather large pair of twins appeared; smiled at Jack and said that they had come for the unhealthy ones.

Jack watched as the twins carried their patients away on rolling beds and as he was about to ask Nicholas what he thought about Chameleon, he noticed someone else from the past approaching

"Nicholas, my friend, how are you?"

When Nicholas heard this voice, he knew instantly that this was the voice of his best friend Peter.

"Surprised, Nick?"

"Of course not, Peter."

"I wake up on an island with no idea of who I am, I find out that I can travel through time then I find out that I'm Santa Claus, and now I find out that my best friend lives on another planet, why would I be surprised?"

"Nicholas, I have been waiting for this day, aren't you even a little bit happy to see me?"

Nicholas saw that Peter was really sincere and in reality, he was thrilled to see Peter again. He remembered the last day that the two of them were together; it was the day he woke up on Bliss.

"Of course I'm happy to see you, Peter, but I had no idea that…"

"I was part of the plan all along?

"Neither did I Nick; that is until I ended up on Chameleon.

At first I thought I had died and gone to heaven."

"I know that feeling quite well."

"Then you must know that I have been through pretty much the same process as you have."

Nicholas laughed as he hugged his friend.

"Well, I know that you're *not* St. Nicholas, so who... no, tell me you're *not* St. Peter."

"I can't tell you that Nick because I am St. Peter, the one and only."

"Since everyone ends up in heaven sooner or later, I guess my job was obsolete."

"I woke up on Chameleon, just like you did on Bliss."

"I was told that I returned to an earthly body to become your friend because the two of us would be working together in order to save humanity."

"Imagine that, Peter and Nicholas, back to back, saving the universe, would you ever have imagined that, Nick?"

"Not in my wildest dreams, but it didn't actually turn out to be little old Peter and Nicholas did it? We are actually the reincarnated souls of saints, go figure."

"So you and Nicholas grew up together?" asked Geoffrey.

"Indeed we did, Geoffrey, and if you'll remind me later, I'll tell you all about little St. Nick."

"You know what, Peter? I'm more interested in you telling me where that voice came from."

"What voice, Geoffrey?"

"The one that said, *welcome to Chameleon, everyone*. I heard him but I never saw him."

"That's because he wasn't actually present when he spoke, Geoffrey, he's in that tower over there."

Geoffrey looked up in the direction that Peter was pointing and said all he could see were rainbows.

"Maybe it's me, but I really don't see a tower, Peter."

"That's because the tower is disguised to look just like the rainbows; in fact you'll find that most everything on Chameleon looks like a rainbow."

Geoffrey shook his head and said he thought he'd seen everything until now.

Peter smiled and asked everyone to follow them to what he liked to call the *Rainbow Resort*.

"I'll show everyone to their quarters, and after you freshen up, we'll have a meet and greet before dinner. Does that sound okay to ya'll?"

"Ya'll? Where did that come from Peter?"

"From some sweet little Magnolias from Mississippi, Nicholas, you'll meet them later."

"Their southern drawl just enchants me; in fact, I am quite taken with one of them in particular."

"Oh yeah, what's her name?"

"Her name is Savannah Christian. Her mother was from Savannah, Georgia and her father from Pass

Christian, Mississippi. Her middle name is actually pronounced chris-g-ann, sort of."

"Wow Peter, your eyes kind of twinkle when you talk about her."

"I thought St. Nicholas had the market cornered on the eye twinkling thing, Nick."

By this time the group had reached the *Rainbow Resort* and Peter said it was time to turn everyone over to the best concierge in the galaxy.

"Mario, please take care of these very special guests."

Very special guests, I will see you soon."

"Mario? Geoffrey whispered to Nicholas "did he say Mario?"

Mario turned and looked at Geoffrey without cracking a smile.

"Yes, he did say Mario, you got a problem with that?"
"Don't have a problem at all Mario, just didn't think it suited you."

"Well you're right, it doesn't suite me but it's what they named me here so I answer to it."

"What do you mean it's what they named you?"

"When I first arrived, I moved around the planet so fast that they began calling me Mario Andretti after some race car driver and I guess it stuck."

"So you just allowed these people to change your name?"

"Wouldn't you if your given name was Clyde?"

Chapter Fifty Four

Nicholas and Geoffrey had adjoining suites so Nicholas unlocked the door between the two.

"I don't know about you Geoffrey, but I could use a hot shower right now. What say we meet in your suite for a cocktail after we get cleaned up?"

"Take your time Nick, you know how addicted I have become to hot showers."

"I do indeed my friend and it's no wonder, considering the way you smelled when I first met you."

Geoffrey laughed and said that he took no offense at what Nicholas said because he too had become quite sensitive to offensive smells since he had arrived in the twenty first century.

About an hour later, Nicholas and Geoffrey were resting on the couch in Geoffrey's suite, enjoying a cold ale from the mini-bar.

"Some things never change, eh Nickie?"

"You mean like no matter where you go in the universe, the mini-bar is always stocked?"

"No, my brother, I mean that no matter what century it is, there is nothing like two friends having an ale together, although cold ale certainly goes down much easier than warm ale"

"Indeed it does, Geoffrey, and sharing anything with you is always a pleasure."

As Nicholas and Geoffrey raised their bottles to toast, they heard a knock on the door.

"Nicholas, Geoffrey, are you there?"

Nicholas opened the door and there stood Peter, looking rather distraught.

"Peter, are you okay?"

"No Nick, I'm not okay, in fact, I really need to speak with the two of you."

As soon as Peter entered the suite, Geoffrey handed him an ale and Nicholas asked him what had him so upset.

"Nickie, I need to return to Bliss with you."

"That's fine with me Peter, but I still don't understand why you are so shaken."

"Nicholas, I understand that only those that are pure in spirit can set foot on Bliss."

"Well St. Peter, I can't imagine why you would have a problem with that."

"Nickie, I'm not up to date on what *pure in spirit* really means anymore."

"Peter, I think that it means that your intentions are good. I know it sounds simplistic, but it makes sense. How can you be at fault if your intentions are good? Besides, I thought you were already in heaven once."

"My intentions are good Nick, but I've never been to heaven because I wasn't through on earth yet."

"I guess that makes sense, but I wouldn't worry too much about whether or not you will be allowed on Bliss, if your intentions are good nothing will stop you"

Geoffrey watched as Nicholas and Peter hugged one another. He knew in his heart that both of these men would be a very important part of his future so he left them to share some much needed time together.

"I'll see the two of ya later Nick, okay?"

"Thanks Geoffrey," said Peter. "You don't really have to leave you know."

"I know, Peter, but you two have some catchin' up to do, besides, I think I smell appetizers."

After Geoffrey left, Nicholas asked Peter what had him so upset.

"You can't be in too much trouble, Pete; after all, you are the main Saint, are you not?"

"Hey, don't believe everything you hear. I'm just a spirit having a human experience, just like you my friend."

"I'm sorry, Peter, I guess jokes are not what you need right now so tell me, what has you so upset."

"Nicholas, I'm on a mission, just as you are, but unfortunately, my cover has been blown and I need to leave Chameleon."

"I don't see where that's a problem Peter, we should be able to leave tomorrow."

"Well, there could be a problem, Nick, because part of my mission involves those sweet Magnolias I told you about and if I leave, they must go with me."

"Peter, just who are these Magnolias you keep talking about?"

"They're research doctors, Nick, and they need someplace to hide. I call them Magnolias because they are from Mississippi, the Magnolia state, but these ladies are probably the most sought after research doctors on earth, which explains why they are not on earth any longer."

"I still don't get it Peter."

"Nick, you know that planet earth has been deteriorating for many years, and let's not even talk about the wars."

"So what does that have to do with the Magnolias, I mean the doctors?"

"Nick, they have information that some very unsavory humans want."

"Such as?"

"Such as cures for cancer, aides, diabetes, you name it."

"So what good would these cures do them? The earth as you and I knew it is gone."

"That's true, Nick; however, there are those that hope to take over once the new world begins again. These people want these cures so that they can control who lives and who dies. They want to play God and make a lot of money while they are at it."

"Peter, we won't let that happen. To begin with, Geoffrey and I will be part of the rebuilding of the new world and if we take the Magno…I mean the doctors back to Bliss with us then they won't be in danger any longer."

"Sounds good when you say it, Nick, but I'm not so sure that Leo would agree."

"Okay friend, spill it, what are you not telling me?"

"It has to do with Leo, Nicholas, I'm afraid I am not his favorite Saint, so to speak. You see, when Leo told me that you were the chosen one, I was so happy because I knew that it meant we would be together again, but as fate would have it, I was assigned to Chameleon and you were headed for Bliss, so during a human moment, I tried to get you reassigned to Chameleon and Leo was not very happy about it."

"I don't understand, Peter, Leo has no ill feelings

about anyone, in fact, Leo is the most spiritual being I have every known. No offense."

"None taken, Nickie, I have always thought of myself as a work in progress and this lifetime is not my last rodeo, I'm sure."

"I think you are pretty evolved Peter, after all, you are St. Peter and you're saying things like *I'm a work in progress* and *this is not my last rodeo*. I'm pretty amazed my friend."

"Well don't be, I assure you that Leo won't."

"Peter, obviously you don't know Leo that well, trust me when I say that he will have no problem with you and your team of Magnolia doctors relocating to Bliss."

"By the way, when did you meet Leo, Peter?"

I didn't actually meet him, Nicholas, Leo sent word to me here on Chameleon that you would be assigned to the Island of Bliss and that is when I tried to have you brought here."

Chapter Fifty Five

As Nicholas and Peter arrived at the meet and greet, they noticed that Geoffrey was surrounded by a group of females.

"I see you've met the Magnolias, Geoffrey."

"I have indeed, Peter, and I don't understand why you said that they were a little on the homely side. I myself find them quite beautiful and if I were not already committed to the most beautiful lady in the universe, I would be quite taken with these ladies."

Nicholas laughed and said that Geoffrey was being mentored by Bliss's resident prankster.

"I take offense to that," said Michael, as he approached the group, "and just who might this bevy of beauties be?"

"They be none of your business, Mikey"

"And certainly none of yours, Geoffrey, especially since you are committed to another."

"Enough you two," said Nicholas. "Michael, please find Charles if you will, and meet me back here, there has been a slight change in plans."

"Certainly Nicholas, ladies, would you mind helping me find my friend?"

As soon as Michael left, Peter introduced Savannah Christian to Nicholas.

"I'm very pleased to meet you, Nicholas; Peter has shared so much about the two of you with me that I feel as if I know you."

"I am pleased to meet you as well. Savannah. Peter tells me you are a research doctor?"

"I am, and I cannot wait to relocate to Bliss."

"Oh? You know about Bliss?"

"Well not that much, but Peter told me it was an island and that I would be able to continue my research there.

Nicholas, I grew up on the Gulf coast so I love the beach and the water, so to be able to continue my research in a tropical atmosphere would be more than I could ever hope for."

"Well Peter, I guess you have taken care of everything on your end, so if you two will excuse me, I need to take care of some things myself."

"It was a pleasure meeting you Savannah. I will catch you later Peter."

"Nicholas, you can't leave," said Geoffrey, "you told Michael to retrieve Charles and meet you back here."

"I know, Geoffrey, so if you will please just stay here and wait for them; I'll be back as soon as I can."

"I don't know, Nick, I am supposed to watch out for you so maybe I should go along."

"Right now I'm not the one that needs looking after, Geoffrey, so please just stay here with Peter and Savannah, okay?"

As Nicholas made his way back to his room, he ran into Charles and Michael.

"Nicholas, where are you going? I thought you wanted to meet with Michael and me."

"I do, but you're going to have to come back to my room with me because I need to speak with Leo first."

"Nicholas, is this about taking the Magnolias back to Bliss with us? Cause if it is, I for one am for it one hundred per cent."

"It is about taking the doctors back with us, Charles. First of all, we don't have room for the ladies in our spacecraft, since we will be taking the four we rescued with us. We barely have enough room for Peter."

"Nicholas," said Michael, "there is no way to communicate with Leo without giving away our location to anyone out there looking for us. I'm afraid you are going to have to figure this one out on your own."

Great, thought Nicholas, *my last mission went awry and my parents had to finish my job and now this.*

Chapter Fifty Six

Nicholas asked Charles and Michael to try and cover for him with Geoffrey.

"I need some time alone to think and I cannot have Geoffrey coming to look for me."

As Nicholas laid his head back on the sofa in his suite and closed his eyes, he knew the best thing he could do at this time was to take several deep breaths and calm his mind. *Meditation is just what I need right now,* he thought, but before he had a chance to relax and free his mind of all the clutter, he heard someone knocking lightly on his door.

Can't even meditate in peace, he thought, as he rose from the sofa and answered the door.

"Nicholas, I'm very sorry to disturb you," said Jack, "but Charles and Michael shared your dilemma with me and I believe I can help; that is, if you even want my help. I do understand if you don't because…"

"Uncle Jack, I try not to let my ego make decisions for me. I welcome any and all help that I can get."

"First of all, Nicholas, thank you for calling me *Uncle Jack*, and secondly, please forgive me for aborting your mission on earth."

"Yes, I have been a little bummed that my parents had to complete a mission that I was assigned to do, but when I think about it now, I realize that we are all in this together and there is no one person responsible for what transpires."

"My initial mission was to rescue many others and bring them back to Bliss, but instead, I brought you back to Leo."

"My parents may have rescued the others; however, I have a feeling that I did exactly what Leo wanted me to do."

"I think you are absolutely right Nicholas, and as far as transporting the doctors back to Bliss, I have an idea that I would like to run by you."

"My friends here on Chameleon will allow me to take one of their ships and I can escort Peter and the doctors back to Bliss."

"What about Charles and Michael, they have no idea where we are in the universe?"

"I will lead and they can lock into my coordinates until we are in a territory that is familiar to them."

"I suppose you saved the day this time, Uncle Jack."

"And you made my day, Nicholas, when you called me *Uncle Jack*."

Nicholas said they should probably get back to the others and let them know what the new plans were.

"Besides, if I don't return soon, Geoffrey will tear this place apart looking for me because he would never dream of looking for me in my room."

"I'll meet you downstairs, Nicholas, but first I need to see a man about a space ship."

As Nicholas and Jack hugged, Nicholas couldn't help but feel like he was a little boy again.

Oh to be that little boy once again, thought Nicholas, as he made his way back to see Geoffrey.

"Hey Nicholas, I was just about to go looking for you."

"Well now Geoffrey, now that I am back, you can relax and enjoy the evening."

"Charles and Michael said that you were resting in your suite and that I should not disturb you because you needed a little time alone. They said that this was a direct order from you."

"They were telling you the truth Geoffrey, I did indeed need some time to re-energize myself and now that I have, I would love a cold beverage."

"Coming up, Sir," said Geoffrey; with a huge smile on his face.

Nicholas felt so blessed to have Geoffrey as his friend and he made a silent vow to never allow anyone or anything hurt him as long as he could help it.

After awhile, Jack appeared and announced to everyone that he would not be returning to Bliss aboard the *Sky King*.

"It has come to my attention that we will have more passengers returning to Bliss with us than we had counted on so I will be piloting a second space craft to accommodate these passengers."

"I ask that everyone returning to Bliss meet Nicholas and I back here in one hour."

Chapter Fifty Seven

As everyone was preparing to board the space crafts for the trip to Bliss, Nicholas asked Jack if he thought it was a good idea to leave Chameleon so late in the evening.

"Nicholas, the sooner we return to Bliss, the better. Our enemies will not expect us to be returning this quickly; besides, if we leave now, we can have Geoffrey home just in time for dinner."

"Uncle Jack, you have only known Geoffrey a short time, yet you know him so well."

Jack just chuckled and told Nicholas that he would see him back on Bliss.

"This is just way too easy," said Michael, as the *Sky King* trailed behind Jack's spacecraft.

"What do you mean, *too easy?*" asked Nicholas.

"Something just seems off here, Nick. Whoever was after us must have some kind of radar that would have picked us up by now."

Charles said that he agreed with Michael.

"I understand they may not have expected us to be

roaming the universe so quickly after losing them because it would make more sense to hide out for a while, but I don't understand why they would take that chance."

"Jack believes the enemy continued on a search throughout the universe after we landed on Chameleon" said Nicholas "and he also said that the universe is so immense that they should be too far away from us by now to pick us up on their radar; however, he did say they may have a few of their ships patrolling the area where we were last seen and if that is the case, we may just be in for the ride of our life."

Michael thanked Nicholas and said that his words were very comforting.

"Don't shoot the messenger, Michael."

"I do not believe he would attempt to shoot you, Nicholas," said Geoffrey, "he knows that he would have to deal with me."

Michael laughed and as he began to explain to Geoffrey what *Don't shoot the messenger* meant, all hell broke loose.

"Hang in there guys, you are in for a rough ride."

"That was Jack, Nickie, and he said we were in for a rough ride. What do ya think he meant?"

"I think he meant that we have been spotted by the

enemy, Geoffrey, and in order to lose them, we will be taking a few detours."

"I couldn't have said it better myself, Nicholas," said Michael.

For the next ten minutes, no one aboard the *Sky King* said one word.

Nicholas, Geoffrey, Charles and Michael braced themselves as the *Sky King* did maneuvers it had never attempted before.

Geoffrey finally broke the silence once things seemed to quiet down a bit.

"Are we still alive, Nickie?"

"I believe I am, Geoffrey, but from the color of your face, I would say that you passed away about five minutes ago."

"Nicholas, this is no time for jokes."

"I'm sorry, Geoffrey, I guess fear brings out the *Michael* in me."

"Hey, I resent that statement," said Michael, "besides, I was about to admit to Geoffrey that I was just as scared as he was."

Charles said that it appeared that the worst was over and that they would be landing soon.

Nichols said that it was impossible for them to be home this quickly.

"We cannot even be in earth's atmosphere yet, Charles."

"That's right Nicholas, but we are landing nonetheless, where, I have no idea."

Chapter Fifty Eight

Claire and Heather had planned a welcome home party on the beach deck for the newest arrivals to Bliss and were about to wrap things up when Leo came out to tell them they may have to postpone the party until the next day.

"What happened, Father?"

"From what I can determine, Claire, things just didn't go according to plan and I'm sure you and Heather can relate to that."

"Yes, we can relate to that, Father, but we both know that you are not telling us everything, right Heather?"

"Claire, I do not believe you have given your Father time to explain the circumstances of what may be taking place."

"Heather, you are such a…"

"Careful sweetheart," said Leo, "there is a parent present."

"Father, I was only going to say that Heather was such a diplomat."

"Right, Claire, don't forget, I know you better than anyone."

"All I can tell the two of you is that everyone is fine. They are spending the night on a planet named Oz."

"Father, you are kidding, right?"

"No Claire, I am not kidding. I will find the two of you later when I have more to report."

"What is this place, Nickie?" asked Geoffrey as they stepped out of the *Sky King*.

"You are asking the wrong person Geoffrey."

"It's called Oz," said Charles. "Though I really don't understand how it got its name."

By this time Jack arrived and asked that everyone stay aboard the *Sky King*.

"Charles, Michael; are either of you familiar with this planet?"

"All I know is that it's called Oz." said Charles. "But I've heard that it is nothing like the Oz that Dorothy visited."

"By the way Jack, how did you know about Oz?"

"I didn't, Charles, Peter said that no one in their right mind would land here so I figured that if we landed here we could ditch the bad guys following us."

"Jack, they said no one in their right mind would land here; do you really believe those beings following us are in their right mind?"

"No I do not Charles; however, I do believe they are

afraid to land on this planet because they believe it is haunted."

"Come on Uncle Jack, haunted?"

"Yes Nicholas, haunted. Your good friend Peter said he would tell us the legend of Oz when we are safe, back on Bliss, but for now, I suppose we should proceed with caution."

Geoffrey mumbled something about not proceeding at all.

"What did you say, Geoffrey?"

"Jack, I just don't understand why we have to leave the ships at all. Why not just wait here until those villains go away."

"Because they won't go away for quite a while Geoffrey; trust me, they will orbit this planet until they feel that we have been taken by the creatures of Oz, besides, I don't believe spirits haunt people or places."

"Bite ya tongue, Jack; if this planet is haunted, ya certainly don't want the spirits hearin' ya."

Nicholas laughed and told Geoffrey to relax.

"Uncle Jack told you he doesn't believe in hauntings, and frankly, neither do I."

"Just don't say I didn't warn ya Nickie."

"I won't, Geoffrey, now let's go see if we can find the Wizard."

"What Wizard?" asked Geoffrey as he walked alongside Nicholas.

"Oh, I suppose you have never seen the *Wizard of Oz* have you?"

"No, Nickie, I have never been here before; how could I have ever seen their wizard? I have met a few wizards in my time though and they are very entertaining indeed."

Everyone began to laugh as Nicholas explained to Geoffrey that the *Wizard of Oz* was a famous movie.

"Its Claire's favorite movie and she said that she remembered watching it every year around Christmas time when she was growing up, so of course she took me to the movie theater on Bliss and I watched it with her."

"What in the world is that?" asked Jack, pointing to what appeared to be a community of some sort.

Nicholas commented that it sure didn't look like Emerald City.

"No it doesn't Nicholas, it looks more like Pee Wee Herman's playhouse."

As Geoffrey opened his mouth to say something, Jack stopped him.

"Geoffrey, it would take way too much time to explain Pee Wee Herman to you right now, but I promise I will tell you all about him later."

"I'll be sure and remind you, Uncle Jack, because

I would like to know who this Pee Wee Herman is myself."

"Oh, Nickie, I'm sure you and Geoffrey will not be that interested in the life of Pee Wee Herman; however, I will share this story with the both of you later, as promised, but right now I feel that we should concentrate on the not so *Emerald City* ahead."

Chapter Fifty Nine

"This looks like an old western ghost town" said Michael as *the group approached a* group of worn wooden buildings.

Geoffrey said he knew what the old west looked like because he watched plenty of John Wayne movies on Bliss.

"Those days were pretty tame compared to my era."

"You are definitely right about that Geoffrey, but at least in your day, you could see the enemy approaching."

"What do you mean, Mikie?"

"Never mind, Geoffrey, just run."

Geoffrey grabbed Nicholas by the arm and everyone began to run toward a building that looked like an old hotel and once inside, Jack advised everyone to keep very quiet.

"Please do not move anymore than necessary," he whispered.

After Jack was satisfied they were safe; at least for the time being, he advised everyone to move to the second level of the hotel.

"I believe we have a much better chance of seeing who is after us if we are on the highest level of the building; which happens to be the second floor."

"But if ya think they are ghosts, then what's the difference if we are on the first floor or the second floor?" asked Geoffrey

"Uncle Jack, Geoffrey is right, what difference does it make?"

"Nicholas, these people may live in what appears to be a town right out of the old west, but they actually live in another galaxy, remember?"

"That's true, Uncle Jack, I suppose this could all be a trick."

"Maybe they really are ghosts Nickie," said Geoffrey

"Or maybe they are just trying to make us believe they are ghosts, Geoffrey," said Jack, "either way, we need to find out, so if everyone is ready, let's head upstairs."

As Jack opened the door to the first room on the second floor, he stopped dead in his tracks.

"I'm not sure that any of you are prepared to see this, but just in case I am seeing things, I want Nicholas to take a look before the rest of you enter the room."

"Uncle Jack, this is beyond believable; in fact, I suggest we leave this hotel immediately."

"Relax, Nickie, I believe I know what is going on, I just wanted to make sure that I wasn't seeing things."

"Oh, you are not seeing things, Uncle Jack; this room is an exact replica of the foyer of the house on Bliss, which tells me that the beings on this planet are messing with our heads."

"Well put, Nickie," said Michael.

"By the way, Michael, what did you see back there when you told Geoffrey to run?"

"I saw John Wayne, Nicholas, and we both know that John Wayne is not in this realm anymore so I figured the best thing we could do was to get away from whatever it was that was trying to look like John Wayne."

"So does that mean we are supposed to run if we see Marilyn Monroe?"

"Of course not Nickie, Marilyn Monroe wouldn't hurt a fly, but the Duke just might hurt us if he thought we were troublemakers."

"Troublemakers, Michael, where is this coming from?"

"Never mind, Nicholas," said Jack. "It's obvious that someone is trying to *mess with our heads* so to speak, and we simply cannot allow it."

"I suggest we return to our ships and leave at daybreak for our return to Bliss. The residents of Oz are making it quite clear that we are not welcome on their planet and I feel we should respect that."

As Jack, Nicholas and the others turned and began

to descend the stairs of the old hotel, something very mystical took place.

"Please do not go," said a voice that came from nowhere. "You are the first visitors that have respected our planet."

"In the past, others have come and wreaked havoc on our planet and our people so we found a way to discourage visitors."

Please do not be afraid, you are welcome on the planet of Oz."

Chapter Sixty

"I'm hoping that everyone heard that," said Geoffrey.

"I don't know about everyone else, Geoffrey," said Jack, "but I certainly heard it and to be honest, I was counting on hearing that voice before we left."

"I heard it, Uncle Jack," said Nicholas

"Uncle Jack?" said the voice from nowhere, "am I to assume that was Nicholas?"

"Yes sir, that was Nicholas and I cannot tell you how happy I am to see, I mean hear you again."

Suddenly a rather large figure immerged with a huge smile on his face and threw his arms around Jack.

"Jackie, my son, I never though I would see you again; that is in this lifetime."

"Did he mean, *my son,* literally?" asked Nicholas.

"Indeed I did Nicholas. Jack is my son and I am so happy that he found his way back to who he really is; in fact, his visit to Oz allows me to feel there really is hope for the universe."

"Father, I truly did believe you had crossed over."

"I did cross over, son, to another planet in the

universe. Do you have any idea how big the universe is?"

"I suppose I don't, Father, but that doesn't really matter to me now. The biggest question I have for you at this time is…"

"I know what it is, Jackie, *where is your mother,* right?"

"So where is my mother, Dad?"

"By now I suspect she is on Bliss, my boy."

"Bliss, why would she travel to Bliss, Father?"

"Pleading your case to Leo, son."

"We heard some pretty awful things about you and your mother insisted on going to Bliss to find out from Leo if those thongs were really true."

"Well, Father, I'm sorry to say the things you heard about me were true and I cannot tell you much I regret…"

"There is no place in life for regrets, Jack; you just have to pull yourself up by your boot straps and move on. The important thing is that you are on the straight and narrow now; you are on the straight and narrow, are you not?"

"Yes, Father, I am on the *straight and narrow* as you say, I just don't understand what you are doing on this horribly bleak planet, acting like John Wayne."

"Oz is not a bleak planet son, it just appears that way.

It's kind of like when Dorothy landed on the Oz in the movie. At first it seemed dismal, but soon it became the most beautiful she had ever seen."

"Right, Father, but I don't see that happening here. All I see is a wannabe old western town."

"With an old wannabe John Wayne, right Jackie?"

"No Father, that's not what I meant, I just…"

"Forget it Jack, remember, no regrets."

"To be honest, Jack, you are right, I am playing a John Wayne type because I loved John Wayne and I loved the old westerns; as a matter of fact, I am having a ball."

"I guess Mother thinks you have totally lost your mind."

"Not exactly Jack, in fact, she sometimes pretends to be Miss Kitty from Dodge City. Sometime she even…"

"Oh please Father, I do not need a visual, in fact I have heard quite enough about you and Mother's little games."

"Very well son, then I shall escort you all to the local saloon and we can get this party started. By the way, the drinks are on me."

"Well Nicholas, I was a criminal and my father is insane so I guess that makes me criminally insane."

"Hardly, Uncle Jack, I think your dad is quite entertaining."

"Entertaining, Nicholas, is that what you are calling it?"

"Welcome to *The Long Branch* everyone," said Jacks father.

"The *Long Branch,* Father?"

"Well what else would I call it Jack, *The Short Branch*?"

"I don't know about the rest of you, but I like Jack's dad," said Geoffrey.

"Of course you do, Geoffrey," said Michael. "He is giving away free whiskey."

"That is not the only reason I like him."

"What other reason could there be Geoffrey, unless he mentioned free food?"

"Michael, I'll have you know that I am a very good judge of character and I feel that Jack's father is a very good person. Not everything is about food and drink ya know."

Nicholas was about to tell Michael to lay off of Geoffrey but he never got a chance. Before anyone had a chance to enter the saloon, it literally disappeared.

"What the heck happened to the saloon?" asked Geoffrey

"I suggest we flee now and ask later Geoffrey." said Nicholas.

Chapter Sixty One

"Slow down Nicholas, it's only a strange fog that appears now and then, just follow me."

"Yes Sir, Mr. Wayne."

"Nicholas, my name is not really John Wayne, it's actually Matt and my middle name is Dillon. My wife's name is, well her given name is Katherine, hence, Miss Kitty."

"I guess given the circumstances, I should be grateful they didn't name me Chester."

"Jack, we wouldn't have done that to you. I actually named you after my favorite card game."

"Black Jack, you named me after a card game, Dad?"

"Relax son, let's go inside and have some refreshments."

Everyone followed Matt into the *Long Branch* and Geoffrey said that he could not believe how much it looked like the saloons in the old western movies.

"Leo told me it was called the *Wild West,* but it seemed pretty tame compared to my era."

"Nicholas, the people in your era were not much more civilized than the cave men."

"I shall overlook that remark on one condition, Michael. I would like for you to lend your bartending expertise to our host, Mr. Matt and get back behind that bar and scare me up an ale."

"Well, Geoffrey, since you called me an expert, I will do just that."

"This is great, Michael, we have never had a professional bartender at the *Longbranch* before."

"And ya still don't have a professional behind your bar, Mr. Matt; you just got ole Mikie here."

"Touché` Geoffrey," said Michael. "I actually deserved that; however sir, I will be happy to offer my services anyway."

"Thank you, Michael, the bar is all yours."

Geoffrey whispered to Matt that Michael really was an excellent bartender but that he did not like to brag on him all that much.

"He tends to get the big head, ya know."

"I understand, Geoffrey, and trust me, this will be our secret."

"Oh it is no secret, Sir; everyone knows that Michael has a big head."

"I heard that, Geoffrey and if I were you, I'm not sure I would be drinking any drinks that this big head makes for you, in fact…"

"Nicholas, do you remember earlier when you said that we should run now and talk later?"

"Yes I do, Mr. Matt, but…"

"Well this time we really do need to run. There is an underground tunnel that will lead us to the area where the space ships are. Do not ask questions, just follow me."

As everyone fell in line behind Matt, Nicholas noticed that the skies were turning black and it sounded as if several trains were approaching.

As soon as everyone was safely underground, he asked Matt what was happening.

"If I didn't know better, I would say that the skies were filled with the worst tornados I have ever seen."

"Well, Nicholas, you would be right because those were tornados, of a sort. I'm afraid that Oz is about to suffer the same catastrophes that planet Earth is going through and there is nothing that any of us can do about it, except evacuate as soon as possible."

"Father, why didn't you tell us when we first arrived?"

"Jack, I had no idea that it would be happening

today; in fact, I thought that it would be at least another three or four months before Oz would be affected."

"The important thing now is that we leave this planet while we are still able."

"I will take what few residents there are on *Oz* in my ships and find shelter on another planet."

"No, Father, you will come with me, as will the others on this planet. Leo is the kindest, most forgiving being I know, and no matter what you may have done in the past, all that matters is that you are pure in spirit at this time and something tells me that you are pure in spirit."

Chapter Sixty Two

Everyone continued to follow Matt through the underground tunnels until they reached the area that the space craft were docked.

"Jack, I think you should pilot the *Sky King* since you are more familiar with the territory."

"Of course Nicholas, but I want my father on board as well."

Nicholas agreed and said that Charles could pilot the other ship.

"How many ships do you have, Matt?"

"We have three, Nicholas, but only two people, other than myself can fly them.

I'm afraid I will not be able to join you on the *Sky King* Jack."

"Michael can fly the third one, Father."

"Then I suggest we move as quickly as possible."

No sooner had the five space crafts left the planet Oz when disaster struck.

"Nicholas, the last ship in line is not on my radar screen," said Jack, "and the news gets worse; there is a black hole directly in front of me and we are all being pulled into it."

"Is there anything you can do, Uncle Jack?"

"Yes, Nicholas, pray."

For about five minutes there was total silence as the *Sky King* became completely engulfed in darkness, then suddenly, the skies filled with light.

"What happened, Uncle Jack, where are we?"

"I have no idea, Nicholas, but it looks as if every star in the Milky Way is twinkling, except for those that seem to be forming a pathway to who knows where. It doesn't really matter though because I still have no control over the craft."

"Look, Jack, all four ships are back on the radar."

"You're right, Dad, and they are lined up directly behind us in a perfectly straight line."

"Looks like we are all headed for the same destination, whether we like it or not so everyone, please hang on because we are about to make a landing; where, your guess is as good as mine?"

Each of the five ships landed at exactly sixty seconds of one another and Jack said that it seemed as if someone definitely had an agenda.

"Yes it does, Uncle Jack, and my guess is that Leo is behind all of this."

"What makes you say that, Nicholas?"

"Look around, we are on an island and we are safe; who else do we know that has that kind of power."

As everyone emerged from inside the *Sky King* the first sight they saw was five limousines, lined up in a circle and Leo was standing right in the middle of them.

"Leo, it was you that brought us back, just as I suspected."

"Welcome home, Nicholas, welcome home to all of you. I had a strange feeling you would be arriving back on *Bliss* tonight so I thought I should be here to welcome you home and to greet the newcomers as well."

"You are quite the magician, Leo," said Matt.

"Oh, I'm not a magician Matt; however, *Bliss* can seem very magical at times."

"So how did you know my name, Leo, we have not been formally introduced?"

"There will be plenty of time for introductions later, my friend; right now there is a *welcome back* party in progress."

"But you were not even expecting us until tomorrow, Leo."

"That is true, Jack, but Claire and Heather had already planned a get-together for your home-coming and when you said you would not make it until tomorrow, I felt that they should have the party anyway; I could not see all that food go to waste."

"Food?" asked Geoffrey.

"Yes, Geoffrey, all your favorites."

Nicholas whispered to Jack and Matt that they may as well just give up and realize that Leo always seemed to know what was going on.

"Oh, and the biggest thing you will have to adjust to is that he appears and disappears almost before your eyes."

"See, he is a magician, Nicholas."

"No, not a magician, Matt, just the most highly evolved spirit I have ever known."

Chapter Sixty Three

"Look everyone!" shouted Claire as the Nicholas and Geoffrey got out of one of the limousines and began walking toward the beach deck. "It's Nicholas and Geoffrey, they are home."

Claire and Heather both ran to meet their husbands and with tears in their eyes, they both uttered the same words almost simultaneously.

"You will never again go on another mission without me."

Everyone began laughing and as the group reached the beach deck, Nicholas introduced the newcomers to the other families on the island.

After the introductions were complete and everyone had a glass of Champagne in their hand, Leo made a toast.

"I would like to make a toast to Nicholas, Geoffrey, Michael and Charles, my wonderful boys, to Jack, my dear friend and to all of the newcomers to *Bliss*."

As everyone raised their glasses, Matt seemed preoccupied.

"Are you looking for Katherine, Matt?"

Startled, Matt turned to look into the most piercing blue eyes he had ever seen.

"As a matter of fact, Leo, I am looking for my wife."

"Relax. My darling; I am here, safe and sound."

"Katherine, where have you been?"

"Hiding out, Matthew; wanted to see if you missed me."

"Well I have missed you. Katherine and I have decided that you must never leave me again."

"Mother, is that really you?"

"Yes. my sweet, Jackie."

"Mother, I asked Leo about you earlier and he said that Father and I should not worry because you were safe, but we didn't realize that you were still here on Bliss."

"Jack, I am so happy to see you and your father. I do hope that your arrival means that the three of us are finally together again to stay."

"As far as I am concerned mother, we are together again; however, we must all remain on the island of Bliss."

"I actually agree with you Jack because your mother and I have been separated from you for too many years and if remaining on Bliss means that we can stay together as a family, then so be it."

"Actually, I do not believe it will be that much of a hardship for you, Matt."

"Leo, Nicholas said I should get used to seeing you come and go rather quickly, but if I didn't know better, I would say you are a hologram."

"A hologram, that is quite amusing, Matt; however, my comings and goings are not that important, what is important is that your family remain together, am I correct?"

"Yes, Leo, that is correct."

"Then I believe I have the perfect solution.

You must know that Bliss is an extremely large island and is growing daily?"

"Yes, Leo, I have heard such stories."

"Then I suggest you start your own community on Bliss, like the one you had on Oz."

"You mean you would actually allow me to have my very own *Dodge City*?"

"Why not Matt, it is not as if you will be having any gunfights, since there are no weapons on the island."

"Leo, I don't know what to say except thank you."

"I shall take you on a tour of the island tomorrow Matt, if that suits you, but for now, I shall bid you all goodnight, and I promise I won't be popping back up unexpectedly until morning."

Chapter Sixty Four

"Nicholas, what is going on?" said Claire as she jumped out of bed "It sounds like a hurricane is coming in."

"I was hoping it was a dream, sweetheart, but I guess that was too much to ask for."

"Especially on Bliss, Nicholas; I think we need to find my father and…"

Before Claire could finish her sentence, Leo was knocking at the door.

"Father, what is going on?"

"Nothing for you to worry about, Claire."

"Father, you are not dismissing me, are you?"

"Of course not, my darling, I'm just saying that there is nothing for you to worry about because everyone on the island is safe, no matter what."

"What does that mean, Father, no matter what?"

Claire, you know there are terrible things happening on earth, as well as other planets in the universe; however, everyone on Bliss I safe because *Bliss* doesn't actually exist in the same realm as the universe."

"I don't understand, Father, are you saying that *Bliss* is not real?"

"Oh, *Bliss* is real Claire, as real as anything else you have ever seen or experienced, it's just that no one else can see our island, except the residents.

I shall explain all of this later my dear, right now I need Nicholas to come with me."

"Fine, but please know that I will remind you to…"

"You will not have to sweetheart, I will remind you, but for now, I suggest you get dressed and join the others on the beach deck for breakfast before the weather worsens"

Claire looked at her father as if she had no idea what he was talking about.

After Nicholas and Leo left, Claire took a shower and as she dressed, she wondered just how many more secrets her father was keeping from her.

I know he loves me and wants to protect me, but he also knows that I detest being kept in the dark. Still, I suppose he has his reasons and he did say he would explain things to me later.

"Heather, you scared the…"

"I'm sorry Claire, I was just about to knock, but you opened the door before I had a chance."

"That's okay Heather, It's not your fault, it just startled me for a moment.

Come in, I was just about to go downstairs for breakfast."

"Actually, I was headed that way myself and wanted to see if you wanted to join me."

"Leo and Nicholas stopped by our suite to get Geoffrey so I knew you would be as alone this morning as I am."

"Yes, my father said he would explain all of this later and I'm sure he will so let's go get something to eat, I am starving."

"That's right, storms always make you hungry for some reason, I forgot all about that."

As Heather and Claire headed toward the beach deck, Claire made a comment that she had always loved storms of any kind but had always felt guilty because they sometimes hurt people and destroyed things.

"This is the first time I have ever been able to really enjoy a storm, knowing that it cannot hurt any of us."

"Yeah, your father said that I shouldn't worry because no one on the island is in danger."

"Didn't you want to know why?"

"Not really, Claire, I was just relieved."

"You have no curiosity, do you, Heather?"

"None whatsoever, Claire, unless it has to do with shopping."

"Good morning, Claire, Heather, you too are quite the giggle boxes this morning."

"Oh, good morning, Ruby, I didn't see you."

"Now how could you miss someone my size, Claire?"

"Heather and I were just laughing about old times and how she was such a shopaholic."

"Yes, and how nosy Claire has always been."

"You too are like…"

"We know, Ruby, two peas in a pod," said Heather, "everyone has always told us that."

"Actually, Heather, I was going to say that you two are like Laurel and Hardy."

"Ruby, did you say Laurel and Hardy, well which one of us is Laurel and which one is Hardy?"

"Look at that storm, you two. Better get out there and have some breakfast before it moves onto the island."

"She's ignoring us, isn't she Claire?"

"Absolutely, but I'm too hungry to worry about it."

Chapter Sixty Five

"Nicholas, Geoffrey, I apologize for disturbing you so early this morning."

"No problem, Leo, but did ya bring any grub along?"

"I'm afraid not, Geoffrey, but this meeting will be quite short and I am guessing you will be able to join your brides for breakfast."

"I thought it best we meet on the waterfall deck, since everyone else will be on the beach deck or on the decks of their cottages, watching the storm."

"Nicholas, I have one more mission for you and Geoffrey before the earth and all other planets in the universe come to the end of their transition. After this mission is completed, I will reveal all of the secrets that the Island of Bliss holds."

"Leo, you know that Geoffrey and I trust you with all of our being and we do not care what secrets the island holds."

"Well, I kind of do, Nickie."

"Geoffrey, I swear, you and Claire are just way too curious for your own good."

"Nicholas, everyone will know the secrets of Bliss, very, very soon; it is just that I would like for you and Geoffrey and of course your wives to know first so that you can help everyone else understand."

"Now, your final mission is perhaps the most important mission of any you have ever encountered. On this particular mission, you will be entering another realm."

"Are you saying that we are going to another world, Leo?"

"Yes, Nicholas, it is in fact another world; however, it is a world that occupies the same space as planet earth so it is actually another realm."

"After traveling through time and space, this really doesn't shock me all that much, Leo."

"Well it shocks me, Nickie; in fact, I am still having a hard time believing I am still alive."

"Don't worry, Geoffrey, you are still very much alive, in fact, you are never going to die; however, if you and Nicholas get stuck in the other realm, well, it will definitely appear to everyone on **Bliss** that the two of you have passed."

Seeing the look of horror on Geoffrey's face, made

Leo realize he would have to explain this to Geoffrey in a different way.

"Geoffrey, remember when you were a knight and many people were killed?"

"I remember that all too well, Leo."

"Okay, well didn't you assume that all these people that lost their lives no longer existed?"

"That is exactly what I assumed, but you are about to tell me I was wrong, I can feel it."

"Not wrong, Geoffrey; just misinformed. No one ever actually dies you see, they just leave their human bodies and cross over into another dimension. They still exist; we just can't see them because they are vibrating at a different frequency than they did in their human bodies."

"So does that mean that Nicholas and I are going to have to die in order to cross over into this other dimension?"

"In a way it does mean that, Geoffrey."

"Oh I do not like this at all, Nickie, not at all."

"Calm down, Geoffrey and allow Leo to finish."

"Geoffrey, you and Nicholas will be crossing over into another dimension just like you went back in time. You were like a hologram, remember?"

"I remember that sci-fi series that Nick and I watched about this guy that could time travel and this other guy was a hologram. Are you telling me that Nicholas and I break into a gazillion particles and then reassemble on the other side?"

"I cannot tell you what exactly happens, Geoffrey, but I can tell you that you and Nicholas have gone through this same transformation in all of your other missions but they have always been in this same dimension. This will be different because you will be crossing over into a different dimension and it is very risky, Geoffrey, I will not lie to you, so if you choose not to accept this mission, I will completely understand."

"Leo, I know that you would never risk anyone's life so this mission must be very important to you."

"Geoffrey, this mission is vital to mankind."

"Than I accept this mission and I will stand alongside Nicholas and protect him with my life."

"Thank you, Geoffrey, now, if the two of you are hungry, I suggest you join your wives on the beach deck for breakfast and meet me back here mid-morning so that I may brief you on your mission."

As Nicholas and Geoffrey were walking away, Nicholas turned to Leo and asked him when they would be leaving on this final mission."

"At dawn, Nicholas, the most perfect time of the day."

Chapter Sixty Six

By the time Nicholas and Geoffrey arrived on the beach deck, the skies over the Island of Bliss were turning dark.

"Well, hello you two; you are just in time to dine with Heather and me."

"Geoffrey and I do have perfect timing, my love."

"Especially when it comes to food."

Heather began to laugh.

"You said that, my darling Geoffrey, not me."

"Oh, I am not ashamed of the fact that I love good food and compared to what I had to eat in my day, all food is good."

"I wouldn't let Molly hear you say that, Geoffrey," said Ruby as she approached the table.

"Oh, hi Ruby, guess you didn't realize that I was about to say *all food is good, but Molly's food is superb.*"

"Good save, Geoffrey, but I am not here to spy on you, I am actually here to tell Nicholas that Jack would like to see him after breakfast if possible. He says it is important; however, it is not urgent."

"I can meet with him Ruby but I don't understand why he didn't come and tell me himself."

"I have no idea Nicholas, I am just the messenger."

"Did he say where he wanted to meet him, Ruby?"

"No, but I assume he wants you to come to his suite because that is where he is now."

"Thank you, Ruby."

As soon as Ruby walked away, Geoffrey asked Nicholas if he thought that Jack was sorry he came to Bliss.

"I don't think so, Geoffrey, I believe he is just distraught about something and needs someone to talk to."

"Claire, do you mind if I skip breakfast and catch up with you afterwards?"

"Of course not darling, just meet me back at our suite when you are done with your meeting."

By the time Nicholas arrived at Jack's suite, the skies were almost pitch black.

"Uncle Jack, are you there?" he asked, knocking softly on the door.

Jack threw the door open so quickly that Nicholas took a step back.

"I'm sorry, Nickie, I guess I'm just a little anxious. I just found out some rather disturbing news and you are the only one I feel I can share it with."

As Nicholas sat down on the couch in Jack's suite, Jack began to pace up and down.

"Sit down, Uncle Jack, what could be that terrible?"

"Oh, it's not terrible, Nickie, just shocking. I just found out from Leo that I have a son."

"A son; that is great news Uncle Jack, but…"

"Nickie, Peter is my son. Your best friend when you were growing up is my son. I was around him his whole young life and I never knew."

Peter's mother and I dated for awhile and suddenly she broke up with me. She said that she had been seeing someone else behind my back for the last few months and they were getting married. I was devastated Nicholas because I truly loved Patrice; however, my pride would not allow me to tell her that not only had I planned to propose to her, but that I had the ring in my pocket when she told me."

"Uncle Jack, I am so sorry."

"Nicholas, Patrice will be arriving on the island tomorrow and I have no idea what to say to her. I feel so…"

"Uncle Jack, why not wait and see what she has to say, there must be a reason she didn't tell you that Peter was your son; maybe she didn't know that he was your son."

"Why did Leo tell you this now?"

"He said there is nothing but truth on Bliss and though Patrice is pure in spirit, she held a secret that would have kept her away from the island. Leo said that by revealing this secret, Patrice would be allowed to come here and explain why she never told me that Peter was my son."

"Then that is your answer, Uncle Jack. Allow Patrice to explain why she hid this from you, if in fact she did hide it."

"What if she doesn't bring it up?"

"She will bring it up, Uncle Jack. I'm sure Leo has informed her that you already know. If she wants to see her son, this information will not keep her away."

"Now I know why I asked you to meet with me, Nickie. I really do feel so much better.

You know, Peter always reminded me so much of me when I was a youngster and I always thought it was because his mother and I had come so close to being his parents. I never dreamed that he was actually mine, but I often wished that he was."

Chapter Sixty Seven

As the hours passed, conditions seem to deteriorate on Bliss; *still, Leo continued to say* that no one would be harmed by this ominous storm.

The only thing Leo had asked of the residents of the island is that they do not set foot on the beach until the storm passed.

After meeting with Jack, Nicholas decided to try and find Leo but by the time he reached the foyer, Leo was waiting for him.

"Guess I should have known you would find me before I could find you Leo. You seem to hear me before I even speak."

"I do not really hear you Nicholas, I just sense that you need me, so you see, you never have to worry that I can read your thoughts."

"Leo, I understand why you told Jack that Peter is his son, but I do not understand why you didn't tell him the whole story."

"The story is not my concern, only truth is my concern."

"Does Peter know?"

"Peter has known for quite a number of years."

"I do not understand, Leo, why has he never shared this with me?

"Nicholas, his mother asked him to keep this a secret, not only because Jack was so involved with his own causes, but because Peter had been raised by a wonderful man that adored him, a man that was on his deathbed."

"Did this man ever know that Peter was not his?"

"He knew, but he loved him as if he were his own son nonetheless."

"You see, Nicholas, there can be no secrets here so I spoke with Peter and told him that Jack deserved the truth. Peter asked that I break the news to Jack because he was a little apprehensive since he had known quite some time. He promised to speak with Jack later today, after the initial shock wears off."

"Leo, I don't think it will wear off. Jack is devastated by this news. He seems to believe that his life would have taken a different turn if he had known that Peter was his son."

"I know he does, Nicholas; however, this would not have been the case."

"Did you tell him that, Leo?"

"I did, Nicholas, but I do not think he was ready to hear what I had to say."

"Jack was a good man, but never wanted to be tied down by anyone or anything, not even Patrice, Peter's mother, so when she found out she was carrying his child, she tried several times to tell him but each time she tried, Jack would bring us his latest cause he was about to become involved in and he would tell her that someday he wanted to settle down and have a family with her but that he just wasn't ready so you see, she finally made the decision to move away and raise Peter on her own because she could not bear to have Jack look at her and Peter and see them as the ones that held him back."

"But she and Peter never moved away, Leo."

"That is correct, Nicholas and that is because the man that became Peter's stepfather stopped her. He had been in love with Patrice for as long as he could remember; however, she had always only considered him her dearest friend so when she announced that she was moving away, he begged her to tell him the truth about why she had decided to leave so suddenly. Patrice did of course share her secret with him, but not without swearing him to secrecy first."

"He of course broke down and told her that he had always loved her and would marry her and give the child his name."

"Didn't Uncle Jack think it was strange that Patrice suddenly got married and had a child so quickly?"

"Nicholas, back then, Jack was so involved with helping everyone else with their cause; he wasn't paying much attention to much of anything else. He was gone for awhile, and when he returned, he found out that Patrice had married her best friend and that they were expecting a child."

"I think he was quite relieved to tell you the truth Nicholas because he did feel guilty that he couldn't provide Patrice the life she deserved."

"Couldn't, or wouldn't, Leo?"

"Nicholas, that is not for you or anyone else to decide. We are each responsible for our choices and whatever reasons Jack had for the choices he made, they were his choices and he alone would have to deal with the consequences."

"But what about Peter and Patrice, didn't they suffer from Jack's choice?"

Patrice had a wonderful, loving husband and a Peter had a father that adored him.

Jack may be a little resentful now, but when he has time to digest all of this, I believe he will see that Patrice made the right decision."

"What about Peter, didn't he resent Jack?"

"I don't think so, Nicholas. Patrice was very honest with Peter and since he was able to be around Jack while he was growing up, I think he realized that the man that raised him was his mother's best choice."

"Still, Jack was his biological father and Peter never let on that he knew."

"Peter has always been an honorable man, Nicholas, and remember; he promised his mother he would never disclose r secret; besides, Peter could see that Jack was all over the map so to speak and do you think he would have traded having a father that was there for him for one that may or may not show up?

Jack will heal from this, Nicholas. Patrice is due to arrive tomorrow and will help with the healing process. Things are as they should be."

"That makes me feel much better, Leo."

Leo smiled as he patted Nicholas on the back.

"You are a very compassionate man, Nicholas; now, I must run, but I will see you and Claire for dinner tonight."

"Your wish is my command, sir" said Nicholas as he winked at Leo and ran off to find Peter.

Chapter Sixty Eight

"Nicholas, where have you been, never mind, where are you going?" said Claire, as she ran into Nicholas in the foyer.

"Claire, darling, I was going to find Peter, have you seen him?"

"Yes I have, Nicholas, he is headed for the beach. I tried to stop him because father said that we would all be safe as long as we stayed away from the beach.

I was headed for father's office when I ran into you."

"Claire, I just met with Leo and I think he is still in his office so find him and tell him that Peter is headed toward the beach."

"What are you going to do, Nicholas? No, don't tell me, you are going after him?"

"Claire, please go find Leo."

As Nicholas ran out the front door, Claire headed to find her father; meanwhile, Geoffrey began running after Nicholas.

"Slow down, Nicholas, I just ate a pretty hearty meal and I cannot move as fast as you."

Nicholas looked back at Geoffrey and he knew it

would be a waste of breath to tell him to go back to the house and wait for him so he just continued to run as fast as he could.

By the time Nicholas reached the beach, peter was standing on the water's edge.

"Peter, don't do it."

"Do what, Nicholas?"

"Don't go in the water."

"I was a fisherman at one time, Nicholas. You cannot tell a fisherman to stay out of the water; besides, the storm is not nearly as close as it seems."

"I don't care how close the storm is, Peter, I just care about my friend. You were the first real friend I ever had and I will not lose you again, understand?"

Peter turned and began walking toward Nicholas, but before he made it halfway across the beach, he disappeared.

"Geoffrey, did you see that, Peter is gone?"

"I did see that, Nicholas, and though I know you are upset about it, I feel that we need to find Leo."

"I agree, Geoffrey, Leo is the only one that can give me an answer."

By this time, Jack had arrived.

"Nicholas, I thought I saw Peter just now; where is he?"

"I have no idea, Uncle Jack, but I'm hoping that Leo does; what are you doing down here anyway?"

"I was standing at my window and I saw you running toward the beach so I came to find out why. I saw Geoffrey running after you so I was afraid that something was wrong. You know you are not supposed to be near the beach, Nicholas, so what is going on?"

"I don't know what's going on Uncle Jack, maybe Leo can explain."

By the time Nicholas, Geoffrey and Jack made it to the front porch, the heavens opened up and the rains began.

Ruby was standing on the porch with towels and said that Leo was waiting for them in the solarium.

"How did you know where we were, Ruby?" asked Jack.

"Uncle Jack, Leo sent Ruby; he always knows where everyone is."

No one spoke a word until they arrived at the solarium.

"Leo, you sent for us?"

"Yes, Nicholas, I wanted to meet with you and Geoffrey once more before your mission tomorrow."

"But what about Peter, Leo?"

"What about Peter, Nicholas?"

"Sir, not to be disrespectful, but you know everything

that happens on Bliss, so I cannot believe that you don't know that Peter disappeared."

"Peter didn't disappear, Nicholas, he is where he wants to be at this time."

"And where might that be Leo?" asked Jack.

"I believe you know the answer to that Jack, Peter is with his mother."

"Is she…"

"No, Jack, Patrice is as alive as you are, and so is Peter; you will see them both tomorrow."

"I cannot believe that Peter would disappear like that, allowing me to think the worst."

"Nicholas, Peter went down to the beach to meditate and his thoughts were on his mother when you arrived."

"But he turned and headed toward me, Leo."

"Yes, but the thoughts of his mother were too strong so he went to her instead.

Jack, I need to meet with Nicholas and Geoffrey briefly; however, I would very much appreciate you joining me for dinner this evening."

"Thank you, Leo; I would like that as well."

Nicholas watched Jack walk away and he knew that Leo had invited his uncle to dinner for a reason. Leo wanted to prepare Jack for his meeting the next day with Patrice and Peter.

Nicholas knew that Jack would feel so much better

after spending time with Leo because that is the effect Leo had on everyone.

I just wonder who Leo really is, thought Nicholas, as he and Geoffrey sat down to hear what Leo had to say.

"First of all, Nicholas, I want you and Geoffrey to know that I am exactly the same as the two of you; no better, no worse and whatever I can do, the two of you can do as well; now that said, we will begin our meeting."

Chapter Sixty Nine

By late that afternoon, the storm was raging and Nicholas and Claire were getting ready to go downstairs and join some of the others for cocktails.

"Nicholas, Father said these storms are *Mother Nature* cleansing the earth as well as other planets so they can begin again. He said she was righting the wrongs that had been done to the planets by mankind. What I do not understand is why Bliss is not affected by these storms."

"Claire, do you even know where Bliss is, for that matter, do you even know who your father is and what kind of power he has?"

"No, Nicholas, I do not know where Bliss is and I have no idea who my father is or what kind of power he has. I have dealt in logic most of my life and now, suddenly I am thrust into this fantasy world."

Nicholas, I met you and we fell in love, then suddenly I find out that my real parents are aliens and that you are a time traveler, not to mention the fact that you are the real *Santa Claus.*"

"I found out that it snows on certain parts of this

tropical island at certain times of the year and the next thing I know is that we are on a mission to save planet earth."

"This is all a little much for one girl to take in, don't you think?"

"I guess if the girl was just a normal girl, I would say yes, this is way too much for her to take in; however, the girl I am looking at is not a normal girl, she is my super hero girl, the one that I have waited for my entire life."

"You do know how to make a girl swoon my darling; care to have a glass of champagne before dinner?"

Leo had arranged for him and Jack to have dinner together on a private balcony overlooking the waterfall.

"Leo, this view is breathtaking."

"Yes, Jack, it is one of my favorite places to come when I need solace."

"Forgive me, Leo, but I cannot imagine you ever needing solace. You have a beautiful wife and daughter, as well as Nicholas for a son-in-law. You have Bliss, and everyone, including me, loves you."

"Jack, my friend, everyone needs solace."

"Forgive me, Leo, I have no right to…"

"Jack, please sit down and have a drink with a dear friend

"Of course, Leo; my dear friend."

"Nicholas, I do believe I heard trees falling," said

Geoffrey as he approached Nicholas and Claire in the main dinning room.

"That could be, Geoffrey; Leo only said that we would all be protected, he did not say that the trees or houses would survive."

"He didn't say that the food supply would survive either, Geoffrey"

"Then I suppose I should do my knightly duty and eat as much of it as I can so that it does not go to waste."

"That sounds pretty logical to me, Geoffrey."

"Thank you, Nicholas; I pride myself on my logic."

"Did I hear logic and Geoffrey in the same sentence?" laughed Michael.

"And what rock did you crawl out from under, Michael?" said Geoffrey.

"Oh, the rocks were much too wet for me to hide under, Geoffrey, so I thought I might join you for dinner."

Nicholas told Michael that he was very welcomed at their table, but as Michael started to sit down, their lights went out.

Nicholas asked everyone to remain calm.

"The lights will probably come back on soon; besides, candlelight is very romantic, don't you think?"

By this time, Claire and Heather had already started lighting candles and as Claire lit the last one, she saw her father standing before her looking like a huge translucent figure.

"Father, how long have you been standing there?"

Suddenly the lights came back on and Leo was nowhere in sight.

"Nicholas, did you…?"

"Yes, Claire, I did see him and now he is gone; well, maybe not gone, but we cannot see him anymore."

"What the heck does that mean, Nicholas?"

"Claire, I believe your father is always present but we only see him when he wants us too. I also believe we see him in the form he feels we are comfortable with, a human form."

"Are you saying that my father is not a physical being, Nicholas?"

"Well, yes, Claire, I am saying that. You saw the same thing I saw when you lit the candles and I will wager that we are the only ones that saw it."

"And why would we be the only ones, Nicholas?"

"Because your father does not makes mistakes, Claire so I believe that you and I are the only ones that were meant to see him."

"Remember when he came to visit us this morning and he said that he would tell us everything after this last mission?"

"Well, Nicholas, I do remember him saying that

he would tell me everything later; however, I do not remember him saying anything about a last mission."

"Oh, yes, I forgot to mention that part; guess I got a little ahead of myself."

"Geoffrey and I are going on one final mission in the morning and…"

Before Nicholas could finish, Geoffrey began yelling something about fireworks on the island.

Nicholas turned to see Geoffrey running toward the beach deck.

"Hurry, Nickie, hurry; I believe the island is on fire."

Chapter Seventy

As everyone gathered on the beach deck to watch the light show, Nicholas and Claire saw the huge translucent figure they believed to be Leo, heading for the beach.

"We are the only ones that see him, Nicholas."

"Yes, we are, Claire and I believe he wants us to follow him. I suppose I should make some excuse to everyone, especially Geoffrey so that we are not followed.

Listen, everyone, Leo was here a moment ago and he asked that everyone return to their quarters."

Of course no one would question Nicholas, except Geoffrey of course.

"Nicholas, what are you up to?"

"Geoffrey, you must trust that I am doing what Leo wants me to do and I will explain everything to you later."

"Of course I trust you Nicholas; however, I will wait up until you return."

"I would not have it any other way my friend."

As soon as everyone had gone back inside the house,

Nicholas and Claire left the beach deck and headed toward the beach.

"Hold up, Nicholas, I am going with you and Claire."

"Uncle Jack? I don't…"

"It's okay, Nicholas, I saw Leo at the same time you and Claire saw him; in fact, I was standing right next to him. He and I had just finished dinner and he said he needed to see you and Claire. He also said that I should join the three of you but by the time we made it to the dinning room, the lights had gone out."

"Claire, I saw you and Heather lighting candles and when you lit the last one, I saw the look on your face. You looked as if you had seen a ghost so I turned and saw exactly what you and Nicholas had seen. I knew it was Leo but he looked like a huge translucent figure and though he never spoke, I knew that he wanted me to follow the two of you."

"I know what you mean, Jack, because when I first saw the figure, I knew it was my father and that he had something to tell me."

"I felt the same way, Uncle Jack; however, I don't believe Claire and I knew what he wanted us to do until we arrived on the beach deck and saw him heading for the beach. No one saw him except us so we knew he wanted us to follow."

"Then let us follow *The Master*," said Jack.

As Nicholas, Claire and Jack reached the beach, they noticed there was a fog that kept them from seeing the water.

"Do not be alarmed, everything is as it should be."

"Leo?" asked Nicholas

"Father, is that you?" asked Claire.

"This fog is simply an illusion and you will see why in a moment," said Leo as he immerged from the swirling mass "Bliss is leaving this earthly realm."

"What do you mean, *leaving*, Father?"

"Claire, Bliss was never meant to be a permanent fixture in the earth's atmosphere; in fact, it was created to be a safe haven for the new residents to make their transition from the past to the future, without all the distractions of life in a typical city on earth in the twenty first century."

"Nicholas and Geoffrey will be making their final journey in the morning to another realm and when they return, Bliss will be in its last stage of transformation."

"But Father, what if....?"

"Claire, darling, there are no what ifs; there are only whens."

"I get it, Father, Bliss is leaving the earthly atmosphere in a certain time frame whether Nicholas and Geoffrey return in time or not."

"Such a smart daughter I have; and you are completely right, my dear."

"It doesn't take very much sense to figure out that if Nicholas and Geoffrey do not return before Bliss leaves the earthly realm, they may be lost forever. I cannot believe you would allow this, Father."

"Claire, I trust Leo and I know you trust him as well. Please have faith that all will be as it should be."

"I do trust my Father, Nicholas, but unless he is God, he cannot guarantee that you will return before it is too late."

"Claire is right, Nicholas, I cannot guarantee that you and Geoffrey will return in time and if that is the case, we may never see the two of you again."

"Leo, this mission must be extremely important or you would not risk our lives so I will be here tomorrow morning as promised."

Chapter Seventy One

As Nicholas and Claire headed back to their quarters, Claire asked Nicholas why her father could not send Jack on this mission.

"Jack has no family, Nicholas, and he has known him for quite a few years."

"Claire, your father has his reasons for sending me and I will not question those reasons."

"You really do have faith in Leo, don't you Nicholas?"

"Complete faith, Claire."

"Then I will say no more my darling and I will keep the faith that you will return before Bliss no longer exists in the earthly realm."

"Thank you, my sweetheart and I will promise to return to you."

As Nicholas and Claire approached their suite, they saw Geoffrey sitting in a chair in front of their doorway, snoring so loudly that Nicholas burst out laughing, causing Geoffrey to wake up and fall out of his chair.

"Geoffrey, it's a wonder anyone has been able to sleep with all that noise coming out of you."

"Nicholas, you scared me."

"You scared me as well, my friend; it sounded like the storm was blowing out every door and window in…"

"Knock it off, Nicholas; I need to know what happened tonight and I will not leave until you tell me."

"Very well, my friend; Leo said that Bliss is leaving this dimension and if we do not return in a timely manner, we will be stuck in this realm without our family and friends, forever; happy now?"

"That is absurd, Nicholas; not even I am that naïve, now tell me the truth."

"The truth is that I am exhausted, Geoffrey, and if we are going to be alert enough to go on this final mission in the morning, we should really consider getting some rest; now please get out of the hallway and into your own comfortable bed and I will see you in the morning."

I suppose I could sit here all night waiting for Nicholas to tell me what really happened, thought Geoffrey as he watched Nicholas open the door to his own quarters, *or I could go inside and get into my very comfortable bed and find out what's going on in the morning, preferably over a huge stack of pancakes.*

"Well Geoffrey, what did you decide?" asked Nicholas as he opened the door to his suite.

"I decided on pancakes, Nickie, pancakes and bacon I think."

Nicholas smiled and nodded.

"See you in the morning, Geoffrey."

"Bright and early, Nicholas?"

Bright and early, Geoffrey."

As Nicholas and Claire closed the door behind them, Nicholas said he wondered how Geoffrey was going to feel when he told him that everything he said to him tonight was the truth.

"Nicholas, Geoffrey loves you like a brother and when he realizes that you were acting on my father's orders, he will forgive you."

"That's just it, Claire, I don't want Geoffrey to have to forgive me; I want to be able to share the information with him that Leo gives to me."

"But Nicholas…"

"I now what you are about to say Claire, you are going to tell me that Geoffrey cannot always handle the truth and you would be right. I told him the truth tonight and he didn't believe me."

"He just thought you were kidding him, Nicholas, but if you told him that you were serious, I really believe he could handle it."

"Claire, I know that Geoffrey could handle just about anything I throw his way; however, Leo asked that I not share this with him until morning and I have to believe Leo's request was for a reason."

"My father loves you and Geoffrey, Nicholas, so I have to agree that his request to keep things quiet until tomorrow must be for a reason."

"So, why don't you and I have a celebratory glass of Champagne, my love?"

"And just what are we celebrating?"

"The present, my darling, the present."

Chapter Seventy Two

"Time to go, Nicholas," said a loud booming voice out side of Nicholas and Claire's suite.

"Geoffrey, it's barely daylight," said Nicholas as he through open the door.

"Ya not even dressed, man, get a move on, I'm starving."

"Fine, but you go on ahead and have your first course and I'll join you for your second."

"Nickie, you know me so well, but I'll eat slowly anyway; wouldn't want you to eat alone."

"Geoffrey, don't worry about me, Claire will be joining us for breakfast."

"Yes, Heather will as well; she was just getting in the shower when I left."

As soon as Nicholas closed the door behind Geoffrey, Claire burst out laughing.

"What is so funny, Claire?"

"Geoffrey, haven't you noticed how he is always

starving the morning of a mission; it's as if he thinks breakfast is the last meal he will ever get."

"Darling, first of all, Geoffrey is always starving, but he becomes a little nervous on the morning of a mission because he feels he is responsible for my safety so he covers up his fear by saying he got up early because he was hungry; truth be told, he has probably been awake for hours."

"Like you, Nicholas?"

"Claire, I never sleep well the night before a mission, you know that; however, this mission is different, mine and Geoffrey's future depends on the success of it."

"But the bright side of this mission is that it is your last one and I have every confidence that you and Geoffrey will succeed, just as you always do."

"And we will, my dear, because we have wives that have faith in us."

"That's right, Nicholas, now let's go have breakfast with Geoffrey and Heather so you can get this mission over with and come home."

By the time Nicholas and Claire arrived for breakfast, Geoffrey was refilling his plate and Heather was sipping on a cup of coffee.

"Good morning you two," said Heather "I was just

about to serve my self at the wonderful breakfast bar Molly set up for us."

"Good, I'll go with you, Heather; Nicholas, shall I fix a plate for you?"

"No thank you, Claire, I'm going to have a cup of coffee first."

As soon as Claire and Heather left the table, Nicholas asked Geoffrey if he was nervous.

"Me, nervous, of course not Nicholas; why I'm as calm as a cucumber, can't ya tell?"

"Geoffrey, I'm nervous too; after all, this is the last mission and perhaps the most dangerous."

I wanted to tell you what Leo said to me last night, but he asked me not to."

"I do understand, Nicholas, and I would never expect you to break Leo's trust; that is why I didn't push any harder last night."

"Well the good news is that you will find out soon enough and you will probably thank me for not telling you last night."

By this time, Claire and Heather arrived back at the table.

"Hey, I guess I'm the only one without a plate full of food so if the three of you will excuse me, I believe I will remedy that."

Just as everyone was finishing breakfast, Claire noticed the air seemed a little cooler than usual.

"Nicholas, is it me, or does it feel a little chilly out here?"

"I believe I can answer that question, my dear."

Everyone at the table looked up to see Leo standing beside the table.

"Father, I am not even going to ask where you came from but I am interested in why the temperature seems to have dropped."

"Claire, Nicholas and Geoffrey will need to come with me now and unfortunately, you and Heather must remain here. "

"I would like for you to tell Heather what I told you and Nicholas last night and as you tell her, I believe you will have the answer to your question."

"Father, you are taking Nicholas and Geoffrey now?"

"Claire, Geoffrey and I will be back before you know it so please do not question your father about this."

"I love you my darling," said Nicholas as he held Claire in his arms, "and I will see you very soon."

"Of course you will, Nicholas, I have no doubt about that and know that I love you with all of my heart."

Geoffrey and Heather looked bewildered as they said their goodbyes.

"I know nothing about this mission, my sweet, and I feel that Nicholas knows very little more than I do; however, one thing I do know is that I will move heaven and earth to return to Bliss as soon as possible."

Chapter Seventy Three

"Claire, please tell me what is happening to our husbands and why Leo would not allow Geoffrey and I to…"

"Heather, my father only allowed me to know last night because I saw him."

"What do you mean, you saw him?"

"Last night, Nicholas, Jack and I saw my father illuminated before us and then we saw him headed toward the beach. We were the only three that saw him so we followed him and that is when he told us that Bliss was leaving the earthly realm and that Nicholas and Geoffrey must return from this mission before Bliss disappeared or they…"

"Claire, please do not tell me that they could be lost to us forever; and just what is this mission all about? I cannot believe that it could be so important that Leo would risk Nicholas and Geoffrey being lost to us forever and why are you not more upset about this?"

"Heather, Nicholas and Geoffrey have no choice in this matter, the future of our children depend on them; you see, father didn't tell me what the mission was about but he did whisper something in my ear before Nicholas and I returned to our suites."

"What did he say, Claire, please tell me now?"

"Heather, he said that you and I are with child and that only Nicholas and Geoffrey would be able to make sure that no harm comes to our children. He said this mission would buy the time needed for Bliss to makes it's journey into another realm."

"But what about Nicholas and Geoffrey?"

"There will be a fine line of time that will allow them to return to Bliss before it disappears."

"Claire, how can you be so calm about this, these are the men we love?"

"Because we are carrying the babies of the men we love, Heather."

"Do you think Leo is telling them about our babies?"

"Heather, I don't even know how Leo knew we were both with child, much less know what he will disclose to Nicholas and Geoffrey."

"Claire, how were you able to keep this from Nicholas?"

"Well, it was quite hard. Last night, Nicholas asked me to have a glass of champagne with him to celebrate the success of the mission ahead of time so I pretended to take a sip and…well you know how much smarter we are then the male species, Heather."

Heather finally let go and began to laugh and cry at the same time.

"Yes, we are smarter and funnier and than they are, Claire, but Geoffrey and Nicholas are the father's of our children and I want our children to know their fathers."

"I want that as well, Heather but I also want them to have a clear head while they are on this mission and my father asked that I not mention this to Nicholas."

"Then why did he tell you?"

"I suppose he wanted you and me to have something else to hang onto."

"Nicholas, Geoffrey, the time has come for me to fill you in on the most important mission of your lives," said Leo, as the three men arrived at their destination.

"By now I'm sure that Claire has shared the information with Heather that I am about to share with you and I'm certain that Heather believes me to be a very cruel being for sending the two of you away at this time. Truth be told, Claire is most likely struggling with this herself but I cannot tell the two of them the whole story at this time and you will understand when I tell you what your mission involves."

"Nicholas, Geoffrey, your final mission will be to rescue your own sons."

Leo saw the expressions on both the men's faces as he continued.

"The fate of your sons lies in your hands because they are not only in this other realm that will be traveling to, but they are also in the future."

"Leo, this doesn't come as a shock to me or to Geoffrey; the two of us have come from the past into the present so there is no way we can be shocked by whatever you have to say to us."

"This is true, Nicholas, and because of this, I feel that I can share this story with you.

You do realize that the past, the present and the future exist at the same time?"

"We accept this, Leo, because you say it is so."

"Good, now I would like for the two of you to picture a time in the future, a time when your sons would be adults."

"Leo, we don't even have children yet; or do we? Claire and Heather are carrying our sons and you have already told Claire; that is the information she is sharing with Heather."

"Yes, Nicholas, what you say is true and now you understand why I could not allow you and Geoffrey to have this information before today. Claire and Heather will be worried about the two of you but if they knew their sons lives depended on the success of this mission..."

"Say no more Leo; just fill us in on the details of the mission, we are ready to go, right Geoffrey?"

Geoffrey looked as if he didn't hear a word of what Nicholas said; he just stood staring into space.

"Geoffrey, did you hear me?"

"I'm afraid he is in shock, Nicholas; let me see if I can bring him back."

Leo positioned himself directly in front of Geoffrey and stared into his eyes.

"Geoffrey, did you understand what I just told you?" he whispered softly.

Geoffrey smiled and said, "Yes, Leo, you said I am going to be a father."

"Do you remember what else I said, Geoffrey?"

"Yes, you said that our mission would be to rescue our sons."

After having said the words out loud, Geoffrey seemed to return to the land of the living.

"Nicholas, I'm going to be a father; you are going to be a father, we are going to be fathers. Good Lord, man, what are we waiting for, we need to get a move on and go save our boys."

Chapter Seventy Four

After Leo explained everything about the mission to Nicholas and Geoffrey, he said that it was time for them to begin their mission.

"Nicholas, Geoffrey, we cannot afford to wait any longer; Bliss is moving out of the earthly realm and unfortunately, there is nothing I can do to stop this or even slow it down."

"Please close your eyes and picture what you believe your sons will look like as adults."

Nicholas and Geoffrey both did exactly as Leo asked and within seconds, they both had very clear images of their sons in their minds and this seemed to cause both of them to relax a bit.

"Please count to ten, slowly and then open your eyes; you will be at your destination and you know what to do from there."

"Nicholas, should I open my eyes now?"

"Yes, Geoffrey, you should definitely open your eyes."

"Nickie, are you sure we are in the right place, it doesn't look like anything I have ever seen before."

"That's because we are in the future, Geoffrey

Remember when Leo said that if we save our sons, we will save the earth?"

"I do remember, Nicholas, I just don't quite understand what he meant."

"I suppose our sons grow up and travel to earth and this must be what earth looks like in the future."

"It is kind of cool that our sons end up being friends, Nicholas."

"Kind of cool, who are you, Michael?"

As Geoffrey opened his mouth to answer, two men approached them and asked if they needed help.

"As a matter of fact we do need help sir; we are looking for our twin brothers. You see, we were all switched at birth and for the last twenty five years, I have believed that this man was my brother and his twin and my twin ended up together," said Nicholas.

"So how did you find out that you were switched at birth?" asked one of the men.

"Because my brother was in an accident and needed blood, so of course I was ready to donate mine, but when they tested it they said that our blood types were different. DNA tests proved that we were not related so we have been tracking our real twins ever since."

"That is a strange story," said the man. "DNA tests are always done on newborns, have been since before you two were born."

"Yes, well somehow a DNA was not done on the four of us because the two of us are not related and though we love each other as brothers, we would still like to meet the other two."

"I understand, Mr…"

"My name is Nicholas and this is Geoffrey."

"Well, Nicholas, you just made your search a lot shorter because there are two men that live nearby that look amazingly like the two of you and guess what their names are?"

"Where can we find them, Mr… I'm sorry; I didn't get your name."

"My name is Saunders, Chief Saunders. I'm the Chief of Protection here and I'm sorry to have to tell you that your twin brothers are in my custody."

"What do you mean, by custody, Chief Saunders?" asked Nicholas. "What did they do?"

"They didn't do anything, Nicholas; they are under my protection so that they don't do anything wrong; do you not know anything about protection laws?"

"Of course I do, Chief; it just surprised me for a moment; so what were they about to do when you took them into custody?"

"They were trying to leave the planet and everyone knows that visitors to this planet are never allowed to leave."

"Chief, do you not know what the word visitor means?" asked Geoffrey "It means traveler, someone that is coming for a vacation or a business trip."

"I know what the word means, Geoffrey, I just don't honor the word in **Captivity**."

"**Captivity?**"

Indeed, boys, that's the name of my town, **Captivity**; did you not know that?"

"I guess not, Chief," said Nicholas, "so; are we allowed to see our twin brothers?"

"Of course you are, Nicholas; just because we have them in protective custody, doesn't mean they cannot see their family and friends, it just means that we are keeping them in **Captivity** where they belong. We need all the bodies we can get Nicholas and we are not about to let anyone leave if we can help it."

"Follow me boys and I will take you to meet your twin brothers."

As Nicholas and Geoffrey followed behind the chief, Nicholas whispered something to Geoffrey.

"Geoffrey, please keep silent because I am going to figure out a way for the four of us to escape this strange planet."

"Nicholas," whispered Geoffrey, *"I have no idea what*

is going on here so whatever you can come up with to get us out of this situation; I will gladly keep my mouth closed."

By this time, the Chief stopped and said they had arrived at their destination.

"Please come in boys and meet your brothers."

Chapter Seventy Five

As soon as Nicholas and Geoffrey arrived inside the building, they knew that something was wrong. There were no bars on the doors or windows; however, there was a strange feeling that led you to believe that once you were inside of the building, you would never be able to leave.

"Nicholas, Geoffrey, I suppose you are wondering how we can contain anyone inside a building that has no bars; well the truth is that we have not had to depend on bars to hold anyone captive for many years and if you were from this planet, you would have known that and you would never have entered this building."

That's right boys; you are stuck here with your twins, just as you wanted to be."

"No, Chief, that is not what we wanted, we wanted to reunite with our brothers, not be held captive with them. You say you are the **Chief of Protection** but in reality, you are just another bully; someone too weak to be a Savior."

"A bully; you call me a bully?"

"That is exactly what I call you, Chief. We have done

nothing to you or anyone else on this planet, yet you choose to imprison us rather than assist us in our quest."

"Your quest, do I really know what your quest is? As far as I'm concerned, you two are up to no good. You have lied to me and that in itself deserves punishment as far as I am concerned, now get moving or there will be no further need for imprisonment."

Nicholas had a feeling that this so called ***Chief of Protection*** was hiding something pretty big.

"You're right, Chief, we did lie to you because we didn't think anyone would believe our real story. You see, we are from the future and these two men you have held here will determine whether or not…"

"Do not feed me this bull, Nicholas, I know who you are and that is exactly why I am detaining you and Geoffrey, along with your renegade sons."

Nicholas and Geoffrey looked at each other in disbelief.

"Did Leo really believe he could pull this off, Nicholas?"

"I suppose he did Chief or else we would not be here, would we?"

By this time, Nicholas and Geoffrey had arrived at their destination and the chief ordered his men to show them to their quarters.

"I believe you and Geoffrey will find the

accommodations quite comfortable, Nicholas; I will most certainly check in with you later to see if there is anything else you need."

"He is laughing, Nicholas, can you believe that?"

"Well, you know what they say about laughing, do you not, Geoffrey?"

"No I do not know what they say about laughing, Nicholas, but I would love for you to tell me because I am so angry that I need to hear something laughable."

"Well, Geoffrey, they say that *he who laughs last, laughs loudest* and we are definitely going to get the last laugh."

"Whatever you say, Nickie, right now I am kind of nervous about meeting little Geoffrey."

"Yes, well I don't suppose after today you will be calling him little Geoffrey anymore."

Geoffrey looked up to see a young man that was half again his size and he looked at Nicholas and said:

"Nicholas, do you think I am already shrinking?"

Nicholas whispered that he did not think so because he was much too young to be shrinking.

"Besides, Geoffrey, you have to remember that we are not only in another realm and another planet, but we are also in the future."

"This is just way too much for me, Nicholas; I need

some rest and some food, but not necessarily in that order."

"Who are you two and why are you whispering?" asked the smaller of the two men.

"My name is Nicholas and my friend's name is Geoffrey."

"Is this some kind of a joke mister?"

"I'm afraid not son, my name really is Nicholas and my friend's name really is Geoffrey and unfortunately we don't have a lot of time to explain much of anything to you except that we have come from not only another planet, but another realm as well. Oh, and we are also here from the past."

"Okay, Nicholas, just what planet did you come from and why are you here?"

"Actually we are not exactly from another planet; you see Bliss is not really a…"

"Did you say Bliss?"

"Yes I did, son."

"First of all, Nicholas, I do not believe you are from Bliss and you really need to stop calling me son because you are about the same age as I am."

By this time Geoffrey was becoming impatient.

"Just tell him who we are, Nickie; I am starving, and from the look on little Geoffrey's face, he is as hungry as I am."

"Tell us what?" asked Geoffrey Jr.

"That I am your father, little Geoffrey and Nicholas is little Nickie's father."

"Stop calling me little Geoffrey, my name is Geoff. You two may look just like our fathers, but we know you cannot be them because they were killed trying to keep us safe. Obviously this is some sort of trick."

"It is no trick, my son," said Geoffrey, "we are truly your fathers."

"He is right," said Nicholas. "We are your fathers and we were sent here by Leo to save you."

"My Grandfather sent you?"

"Yes, Nicholas, your Grandfather sent us and we do not have very much time to make sure you two are safe or we may never make it back to Bliss before it passes into another realm."

"I cannot handle any more of this on an empty stomach, Nick."

"Geoff, is that all you think about, food?"

"Yeah, they are our sons alright, Nicholas; yours is always asking questions and mine is always hungry."

Nicholas Jr. began to laugh.

"You two do look very much like I remember my father and my uncle Geoffrey, and little Geoffrey most certainly has his father's appetite so why don't we grab a bit to eat and you two can tell us your story."

Chapter Seventy Six

After Nicholas explained everything to his and Geoffrey's sons, he asked that they consider the fact that their mothers were back on Bliss at this very moment looking forward to their birth.

"Boys, I know that you remember so much more than I have even experienced yet in your lives and I believe I speak for Geoffrey when I say that I do not want to know what your life was like growing up; we just want to know that you had a good childhood. I believe the two of us need to experience firsthand what it was like being your fathers when you were children."

"We had a wonderful childhood, Nicholas; sorry, it is quite hard to call someone Father that is the same age as you are, and for the record, I am now called Nick and little Geoffrey is still called little Geoffrey."

"What are you talking about man, I am called Geoff, not little Geoffrey."

By this time Nicholas and Geoffrey were laughing so

hard that their sons both took a step back and looked at them as if they finally recognized them.

"I'm just kidding you, Geoff; let's go feed these two hungry travelers."

"I'm all for that, Nick, and for the record, I knew you were kidding."

As Geoff and Nick led the way, Nicholas and Geoffrey followed, shaking their heads and grinning from ear to ear.

Obviously these two were very much like their fathers and though Nicholas said he didn't want to hear about his son's childhood, he couldn't help but wonder if it was as magical as he had planned for it to be.

As everyone sat down to a meal of leftover meatloaf and mashed potatoes, Geoffrey commented on how some things never change.

"I had meatloaf and mashed potatoes for the first time on the island of Bliss and it has been one of my favorites ever since."

"Mine too, why I remember…"

"I am so sorry to interrupt, Geoff, but we really do have so little time to do what we need to do here and return to Bliss before it crosses over into another realm. If Geoffrey and I don't return in time, you two will grow up without fathers."

"What can we do to help?" asked Nick.

"I need to now where the two of you were headed when you ended up here."

"Oh, that's easy; we were headed back to Bliss to be with our families."

"You mean us?"

"Yes, you and our new wives, who by the way, are also carrying your grandchildren."

"Okay, that does it Nick; we must leave this planet and this realm as quickly as possible or else there will be no future for any of us."

"Now it seems that this **Chief of Protection** character has an agenda; do you know what it is?"

"Not really, Nicholas," said Nick. "I have no idea how we even got here. Geoff and I were going to surprise our wives with these beautiful Christmas ornaments that we saw when we were on Christmas Island. Both our children's births are scheduled very close to Christmas so we decided to take a short trip and bring these ornaments back to hang on the tree; but somehow we ended up on this planet, wherever this planet is and in the city of Captivity. Seems a little far fetched doesn't it?"

"No more so than some of the things that your father and I have been through, Nick," said Geoffrey "I'm sure you heard all those old stories."

"I'm sorry, Geoffrey, but we really do need to get out of here as quickly as possible so our sons are safe back on

Bliss, in the past of course, and we need to be back before Bliss leaves the realm it was in when we left."

Nick said that he didn't know what he and Geoffrey could do to help because they had been held captive for at least a month and had tried every way they could think of to escape.

"It's like there is this invisible shield that keeps us inside this building and Geoff and I have used our mind power to try and escape but nothing seems to work."

"Maybe that is why Leo sent us to help you, Nick; maybe this particular mission takes the power of four."

"Hey, I'm game, Pop."

"And I like the fact that you are calling me Pop, but it sure does make me feel old."

"That's because you are the same age as I am, Pop, I mean Nicholas."

"Pop is fine, Nick, I think I must have earned it along the way; now let's get moving or the four of us may just cease to exist."

Chapter Seventy Seven

"Geoffrey, I'm afraid we may have to dine later, after we get these two back home to their wives and our future grandchildren."

"That is one of the few things I will miss a meal for, Nicholas; let's go."

"What's the plan, Uncle Nicholas?" asked Geoff.

"We move as close to the front entrance of this building as possible, Geoff," said Nicholas with a big smile on his face.

Geoffrey knew that Nicholas was smiling because Geoff had just called him Uncle, at least as far as he could remember.

"As soon as we near the front entrance, the four of us will join hands and picture Bliss. The reason I want you all to picture Bliss is because Bliss is the only place we can all visualize together; the power of four, remember?"

Nicholas, Geoffrey, Nick and Geoff moved through the corridors as quickly as possible until they reached the front entrance of the building.

"Dress rehearsal is over guys, it's time to focus on **BLISS!!!**" said Nicholas.

Geoffrey felt as if this was a scene from Camelot as he watched his son, his best friend and his best friend's son join together and use their powers for the good of all mankind."

This is better than Camelot, thought Geoffrey, as he joined hands with Nicholas, Geoff and Nick. *There is more love and understanding among the four of us than there ever was among anyone in that era because no one understood what life was really about.*

"Shall we join hands?" asked Nicholas as the four men reached the entrance to the building.

"By all means," said Geoffrey.

Each one of the four men had a clear picture of Bliss in their minds. Nicholas visualized not only the beauty of the island but sharing sunsets on the beach with Claire.

Geoffrey visualized how peaceful the island felt after living in so much chaos; he also visualized all the new and wonderful foods he had eaten on the island of Bliss.

Nicholas Jr. visualized the huge Christmas tree that his Grandfather Leo had in the main house every Holiday season and he pictured the snow that came magically to Bliss every Holiday Season.

Geoffrey Jr. visualized the wonderful cookies he left for Santa on Christmas Eve and how he would slip downstairs to sample a few of them before Santa arrived; but the one thing they all visualized at the same time was Claire and Heather and that visualization was the one that set them free.

Soon the four men felt as if they were hurling through space and then suddenly everything was still and quiet.

"Where are we Nicholas?" whispered Geoffrey.

"I have no idea, Geoffrey, but it doesn't look much like Bliss, does it?"

"Not the way I remember it, Nicholas."

"This is not Bliss, Pop," said Nick Jr. "Bliss was always a beautiful Island; no, this is definitely someplace that none of us wants to be."

"I agree, Nick, but if we are not on Bliss, where are we?"

Chapter Seventy Eight

"Listen," whispered Nicholas, "do you hear that?"

"Yes," whispered Geoffrey, "sounds like a tidal wave."

"That is exactly what it is, Geoffrey; everyone run like your life depends on it."

Before Nicholas could finish his sentence, Nicholas Jr. and Geoffrey Jr. grabbed their fathers by the arm and began running so fast that Nicholas and Geoffrey felt as if they were floating on air. By the time the four men touched ground again, Nicholas and Geoffrey were reeling.

"What just happened, Geoffrey?"

"I suggest you ask our sons, Nicholas."

Nicholas Jr. spoke up and said that they had been in similar situations before and their instinct taught them to move as fast as their minds could take them.

"You mean your feet, right Nick?"

"No, Uncle Geoffrey, I meant our minds; now, unless the two of you want to experience another tidal wave, I suggest we get off of this planet."

"I agree, Nick," said Nicholas. "I think we should try this visualization one more time, but this time I will lead everyone in the meditation."

Nicholas asked everyone to clear their minds and relax.

"I ask that you think of Bliss as the beautiful, tranquil island we all remember. Picture the clear blue skies, the clear turquoise water and the palm trees swaying in the breeze, except during December."

"Remember how the island transformed into a winter wonderland? We would go snowmobiling and build the goofiest snowmen we could imagine?"

"We remember this, Uncle Nicholas, but how can you remember it when it hasn't even happened yet for you?"

"You are right, Geoff, I should not remember this, but somehow I do, so I suggest we take advantage of these memories and will ourselves back to Bliss."

"Wait a minute Nicholas, our sons cannot return to Bliss with us unless we return to Bliss in the future and if we return to the future Bliss we will be stuck there."

"You are right, Geoffrey; Leo said that we must return to Bliss before it leaves the realm completely which means we cannot travel to the future Bliss. I'm afraid you boys will have to return home without us and we must take our own journey."

"Nicholas, we must make it back in time or how else could our sons have remembered growing up with us as their fathers?"

"I suppose if we don't make it back to present day Bliss in time, our sons will return to future Bliss with no memory of us whatsoever. I am only guessing, Geoffrey; however, we will ask Leo this question when we get home."

"Now if everyone is ready, we must each picture Bliss as it was when we left it; Nick and Geoff, you must picture your wives standing on the beach awaiting your return and we will picture our wives waiting for us as well; now, are you all ready?"

As the four men closed their eyes and visualized their destination, something very strange began to happen. Though not one of the four was touching one another, they all felt as if they were attached to each other by their fingertips and no one could open their eyes or speak a word. They felt as if they were floating on a cloud in a circle and all they could do was wait until they landed somewhere.

Nicholas felt as if he had been in suspended animation for hours and wondered if the others were experiencing the same thing.

Geoffrey wondered if they were still alive and Geoff

and Nick were just hoping that whatever was happening, everyone ended up on the Bliss they each left behind.

"Are you alive, Nicholas?" asked Geoffrey, as he slowly opened one eye. "I know I'm alive because I am talking."

"We are all alive, Geoffrey and still together, I might add."

Geoffrey opened both eyes and saw Nicholas, Nick and Geoff standing before him.

"Am I the only one that thought we were dead?"

"Pretty much, Pop."

Geoffrey said he didn't care if he was the only one that was scared because it was worth it to hear his son call him Pop, one more time."

"Pop, I didn't say that we weren't scared, I was very scared, if you must know, and to be honest, hearing your voice again was very comforting to me."

"Really, son?"

"Really, Pop"

Nicholas and Nick looked at each other and smiled, but before either one had a chance to utter a word, Leo appeared.

"Well I see you returned to Bliss before it completely left the realm and I see that you saved your sons, now I want to know why you brought them back in time with you.

"Grandfather, you look the same age as when I saw you last and you were at least twenty years older; how did you manage not to age?"

"It is wonderful to see you again, Nick."

"I'm sorry, Grandfather, it really is great to see you again; I was just…"

"I know, Nick, and it is wonderful to see you but you and Geoff cannot be on Bliss at this time. I presume you both know that your mothers just found out that they are expecting the two of you, so of course we cannot risk them meeting you now, can we?"

"No, Grandfather, but what can we do? We have tried twice to return to future Bliss."

"Well, I suppose the third time will have to be a charm or the two of you will cease to exist."

Chapter Seventy Nine

"Father, where are you?"

"Nicholas, you and Geoffrey must take your sons to the Terrarium, now."

As Nicholas, Geoffrey and their sons headed toward the Terrarium, they could hear Claire call out again.

"Father, has Nicholas returned?"

"Claire, darling, I was just on my way to find you."

"What is it, Father?"

"Nothing, really, I just wanted to tell you that Nicholas and Geoffrey should be returning soon."

"Father, really, that sounded so lame, especially coming from you. You would never come looking for me just to say Nicholas should be home soon, now, please tell me the truth, I can handle it and you know this."

"I know you are strong, Claire, but you are…"

"Yes, I'm expecting your grandchild and that makes me stronger than ever so give it up, Pop."

Leo chuckled and mumbled something about being defenseless when it came to his daughter.

"Claire, you know that I would never have sent

Nicholas and Geoffrey on a mission when I knew that Bliss was leaving this realm, unless it was extremely vital to our future, do you not?"

"Of course I know that, Father. I cannot imagine anything being important enough that you would risk my husband's life; however, Nicholas assured me that this mission was that important so I had to trust that."

"Very well, my darling, then I shall explain everything to you."

"I don't believe that will be necessary, Leo," said a very familiar voice.

"Well, well, well, if it isn't my old friend, Nigel," said Leo. "It is wonderful to see you. How is your beautiful wife?"

"Loraine is doing very well thank you, and Ciara?"

"Ciara is perfect as always, but what are you doing here, my friend?"

"Helping an old friend out, I hope, but before we get into that, I just want to step back and look at Claire Bear."

Claire looked confused, so Nigel explained that he knew her when she was just a baby and that he and Loraine had a pet name for her, *Claire Bear.*

"I remember that, Father. I remember a lady with long raven hair leaning over me, calling me *Claire Bear.*"

"That still doesn't explain why you are here Nigel."

"You're right, Leo. The truth is that I heard that Bliss was moving into another realm and that you were experiencing some problems so I wanted to see if there was anything I could do."

"So many years have passed, Nigel, why have I not heard from you?"

"Because I became someone that you would not have been very proud of, Leo."

"And Now?"

"I have a wonderful life on the planet of *Forgiveness*, maybe that is why I have come here at this time. I wish to be of service to you, for a change."

"He is telling the truth, Leo"

Claire turned to see Nicholas walking toward her.

"Nicholas, when did you arrive, where is Geoffrey?"

"Geoffrey is probably with Heather by now and I am exactly where I belong; with you, my love and I promise to never go away again."

"Leo, if you don't mind, I would like to speak with Claire alone, Nigel will explain everything to you if that is okay with you."

"By all means, Nicholas, you two deserve some privacy and I'm sure you could use some rest."

As Nicholas walked away, Leo asked Nigel if it was

safe for him to be on Bliss, while the planet was moving into another realm."

"Leo, Forgiveness is in the same realm that Bliss is heading into so I am safe here.

"Then I suppose this calls for a reunion toast."

As Nigel followed Leo back to the main house, they chatted about old times and Nigel made a comment about Leo not having aged a bit since he last saw him and Leo said that Nigel looked wonderful as well.

"I'm serious, Leo; you really don't look a day older than you did twenty years ago, what's your secret?"

"No secret, Nigel, it's just in the genes, now let's have that toast, shall we?"

"Molly, this is Nigel, a very dear old friend. Will you please have a bottle of champagne and some appetizers sent to the waterfall deck for the two of us?"

"Right away, sir; and it is wonderful to meet you, Mr. Nigel."

"Just Nigel, Molly, please just call me Nigel."

Chapter Eighty

As Nicholas and Claire approached the beach deck, Claire asked Nicholas why Nigel had arrived so suddenly and why he was really here.

"I'm not really sure, but I believe it has something to do with our son, Claire."

"Nicholas, did you say *our son?*"

Nicholas asked Claire to sit down and he began to explain everything that had happened to him and Geoffrey since he last saw her. By the time he had finished, all Claire could say was, *"I'm a grandmother?"*

Nicholas burst out laughing.

"I'm a grandmother, is that all you can say?"

"What do you expect me to say Nicholas; I have not even become a mother yet and suddenly I'm a grandmother. Where is my son now Nicholas, is he safe?"

"Yes he is safe, Claire and he is on Bliss."

"On Bliss, I need to see him?"

"You cannot see him my darling," said Leo, as he

walked out onto the beach deck "Nigel has taken him to the future, where he belongs."

"How could you not allow me to see my own son?"

"Because you are carrying your son, Claire, and the two could not be with you at the same time. Nicholas could be with him, but you could not because he is with you already."

"Yes, he is with me, Father. I feel him, even more now than before and it is comforting to know that he is well and happy."

"And that he is with my son, your God child?"

Claire turned to see Heather walking toward her.

"Yes, Heather, that is a comfort as well."

Soon the skies lit up with colors that were unlike any the residents of Bliss had ever seen and when it appeared to Leo that they had completed their transfer into another realm he asked that everyone take a moment to appreciate life

"All of you have been through many trials in your lifetime but you ended up on Bliss for a reason and that reason is about to be shown to you."

"This will be a spiritual awakening for you and you will be filled with love, unlike any feelings of love you have ever known."

"I welcome you to the Island of Bliss, as you have

never seen it before and I invite you to take this journey with me, a journey of many lifetimes."

Suddenly, Nicholas realized that Leo was the spirit of *Bliss;* that he created *Bliss* with his mind and made it his reality.

No wonder he can never leave thought Nicholas *if he were to ever leave Bliss, it would simply cease to exist.*

Prelude

There is another journey; a wonderfully spiritual journey. One that is filled with laughter, love, adventure, excitement and, well what more could you ask.

There is another journey!